D0754093

"Love is the one ingredient I don't want in my marriage."

Hudson had changed from the pleasant, if annoying, smiling conversationalist to a granite man with a hard expression and challenging, cynical eyes.

"Why not?" Serenity felt absurdly shaken. "Why not love?"

"Been there, done that, next question." His voice was harsh.

"Don't be flippant. What do you mean? That you've been in love and it didn't work out? Perhaps she wasn't the right girl."

"Oh, yes, she was the right girl. I built this house for her. Don't you think it's a nice house?"

"Yes, I do," Serenity said uncertainly. "Why didn't you marry her, if she was the right girl?"

"She died," he replied flatly.

Lake Haupiri Moon

Mary Moore

Harlequin Books

TORONTO • NEW YORK • LONDON
AMSTERDAM • PARIS • SYDNEY • HAMBURG
STOCKHOLM • ATHENS • TOKYO • MILAN

Original hardcover edition published in 1983
by Mills & Boon Limited

ISBN 0-373-02686-2

Harlequin Romance first edition April 1985

For Malcolm Wallace and his wife Noeline,
who own the Lake Haupiri Station and
gave me
permission to use it as a setting for this book.
And thanks also to their children, Ian, Beverley and
Graeme, whose place for the
purpose of this book
has been usurped by the entirely fictitious character,
Hudson Grey.

Printed in U.S.A.

CHAPTER ONE

HIGH up in the Nurses' Home, Serenity James sat on her mattress in the late afternoon sun. Her bed was stripped, her cupboard and wardrobe empty, her luggage packed in her small Mini, because today she was leaving town. Her wedding gown, starkly simple, hung on a white satin-padded coathanger, and in her hand was a photo of John.

She wished she had not told Barbie that she would wait until she came off duty to say goodbye, but Barbie had insisted, and she had been her good friend. That's why she had chosen her to be bridesmaid, and what a fuss that had caused . . . not quite suitable. But according to Mrs Bellamy nothing about Serenity James was suitable, not herself, not her friend, not her accent, not even her mother.

She looked at John's photo. What a handsome boy he was! Why did she still think of him as a boy? He was twenty-five, a grown man. Poor John, he had loved her, but had not been strong enough to stand the pressure. Serenity had chosen this particular photo because it didn't accentuate his weak chin and self-indulgent mouth.

Idly she turned it over and read the verse he had written on the back.

> *Serenity James is tall and slim,*
> *Serenity James has an enchanting grin,*
> *Serenity James has a figure divine,*
> *And Serenity James is mine . . . all mine.*

Serenity looked at the pair of hospital scissors which she had left on the top of the dressing table. Before she left, she meant to cut her wedding dress into tiny bite-sized pieces, and the photo of John, too. But she couldn't bring herself to the point of making the first slash. It was such a lovely dress, and she had looked rather splendid in it. She hadn't chosen the material, she hadn't chosen the style, Mrs Bellamy had even chosen the boutique where it had been sewn. Mrs Bellamy was very organised. Mrs Bellamy was a pain!

Barbie burst in at the door. 'Oh, Serenity, you waited. I was sure you'd take off, and the hurrieder I went, the behinder I got.' She collapsed on the bed. 'Oh, I'm going to miss you so much.'

Serenity smiled at her friend. 'You've got Robbie, you'll make out.'

'I hate this town,' Barbie said fiercely. 'I won't live here when I marry. The Bellamys think they own it. If John had just stuck it out, but he's so gutless.'

Serenity grinned. 'I didn't choose him for his guts, as you so delicately put it. I chose him because he was charming and sensitive and shy, and I knew he was weak—I've always known that. I just loved him, and tried to protect him. I don't blame him one bit.'

'Well . . . I do. To walk out on a girl like you, because Mummy told him to.'

'You forget Mummy had been conditioning him for twenty-four years before he met me. She was in on the ground floor, so to speak, and she had already chosen the wife for him. John stepped right out of character when he started going round with me. He took her head-on for the first time in his life, and it must have been a nasty shock for her.'

'It didn't last long,' Barbie said with a significant sniff.

Serenity smoothed her faded jeans over her knees,

picking a thread. 'Give him his due, Barbie. It was a whole new experience for him. She is the power behind the throne in the family. Mr Bellamy may be Mayor of the town, Chairman of the Businessmen's Association, and all the rest, but she has the brains and the drive, and everybody knows it. He knows he'd be nothing without her; she is a strong determined woman. John couldn't grow up in that atmosphere and not be affected by it.'

'You're still making excuses for him,' Barbie accused.

'Yes,' Serenity admitted with a smile. 'I guess I always will. He is just so nice, and so helpless. If we had married I would have sat back and made him take decisions, made him feel *he* was head of the outfit. He'd have grown to fit the part, but it was tough enough going until my dearly beloved father put in his once-in-a-lifetime appearance. Then it was all over.'

'You're so calm about it all. Today was to have been your wedding day, and you sit there all forgiving . . . you make me cross. I'd have been out for blood. Your mother named you well—are you as serene inside as you are on the outside?'

'What an indelicate question,' Serenity replied. Then added honestly, 'Not quite. I'm still a bit staggered—it all happened so suddenly. I'll get away on my own for a while and sort myself out.'

'I'd sort John's mother out,' Barbie said bitterly. 'Not to mention John himself. Oh, Serenity, do you still love him? Oh, I'm a crass stupid beast! If Robbie left me, I'd kill myself.'

'You won't have to, Robbie is just as besotted as you are,' Serenity comforted her. Then she sat staring out of the window for a moment in silence. 'Love John? Yes, I guess I do. And I hurt for him. He made such a brave showing, and now he must be feeling awful. She actually

made him use the ticket we had for our honeymoon—
Australia, Hawaii, Fiji. Imagine doing those places on
your own when you'd planned to share it with someone
you loved. She must have been completely insensitive to
force him into it, and it will just make him think of me all
the more.'

'Why don't you think of yourself instead of John?'
Barbie said fiercely. 'You've been hurt, too.'

'Habit, I guess.' Serenity brushed her fair hair back
from her pale face. 'I've watched out for him ever since
we met, trying to protect him from the power maniac
who ruled his life, and ours wasn't a wild passionate
affair—not like you and Robbie. John and I were
friends, we sort of drifted together. I was so close to my
mother that I really did not need anyone else in my life.
You're the only true friend I have . . .'

'Rubbish,' Barbie interrupted. 'You've got loads of
friends, everyone likes you. You were the most popular
girl in our class.'

Serenity waved her hands in protest. 'I didn't mean
poor unlovable lonely me, you ninny. I like people, and I
get on well with most of them, but I really only needed
my mother. She was so young, such fun to be with, that I
hardly bothered with my own age group. Then when I
went to Nursing School you and I hit it off right from the
first day, and that was fantastic. What I'm trying to
explain is how John and I became friends . . .'

'Oh, that's easy to understand. He was in hospital
when your mother was killed. You were specialing him,
and he was kind and sympathetic, and when he got
better, he filled up that gap in your life . . . well, he
helped. We *all* tried to help. I loved your mother too,
she's the reason I came here with you when we finished
training. She was a pet, treating me like another daughter. But John had an inside track, you were nursing him

on nights and he got close to you. That's what I can't understand now. How could he hurt you like this? I could kill him.'

'With your temper, New Zealand will never have to worry about over-population,' Serenity offered with a grin.

'Don't side-step the issue,' Barbie burst out, jumping to her feet. 'I won't forgive him for this. I don't see how you can! He should have stood up for you that night, and he just wilted. If he'd been a man, he would have punched that man who said he was your father, right in his mean miserable mouth.'

'Who said he wasn't my father?' Serenity replied carefully.

'What sort of a man was he? To wait twenty-one years, then come full of venom to your pre-wedding dinner and announce that while you used his name you were not his daughter, that you were the reason for his marriage breaking up all those years ago. And he didn't even know your mother was dead. He wanted to hurt her, too.'

Serenity did not answer.

Barbie raged on, 'In front of all the toffs in the town, he almost accused your mother of adultery and rubbished you, and John did not defend you. He just stood there like a stuffed dummy, and then his mother ordered him to his room, and he went like a lamb.'

'She told him she would handle it,' Serenity answered quietly. 'She had always directed his life before I came on the scene, so he automatically obeyed her. He was frightened.'

'Who wasn't? I was terrified. That man was roaring drunk, and so angry that everyone was scared. Yet you walked right up to him and gave him the only answer possible. I'll never forget his face when you said that you were so glad he wasn't your father, and that you admired your mother for making a better choice.'

'It was a terrible thing to say,' Serenity said in a low voice. 'I wish I had asked him to talk to me in private. He turned and ran out and I don't even know where he came from or where he went to. He had all that anger and bitterness locked inside him all those years and it exploded on him. I'll bet it didn't give him half the satisfaction he thought it would.'

'You're incredible! What does it take to make you hate someone? He has ruined your life, and you're trying to make excuses for him.'

'Not really. You didn't see his face when I spoke to him. He was ashamed . . . he just crumpled.'

'But you think what he said of your mother. Where's your loyalty? Did she ever mention him?'

Serenity shrugged her slim shoulders. 'Yes, she said she was married. She said that he left her before I was born. I was never curious about him, I never missed having a father. That sounds silly, I know, but I had a wonderfully happy childhood, and I was perfectly happy with just one parent.'

'But when you were older? Didn't you ask questions then? You had such a wonderful relationship with your mother, surely she could have confided in you, trusted you?'

'She did. She offered to tell me and I said I had no interest in it. She said he had walked out on her, and that it was all her fault and that he was a very good man, and she had hurt him badly. Her own family had been so angry with her, and she had been so ashamed that she moved up here to the North Island and started a new life for herself. I could see it was tearing her apart to discuss it, even so generally, and I did not want to hear the details. What was it to me? I had never met any of the people. I would not have her humiliate herself in front of me. Whatever she did had not been done lightly, and she did not have to explain herself to me. She was my mother, had always loved me and cared for me, and I loved her, and that's all that mattered.'

'But aren't you curious now?'

'I don't know. If I am, it's too late. Among her papers was a large envelope marked, 'Burn without opening', so I did. If she were alive now, or if she had envisioned this happening, she would have prepared me for it. Apparently it was sheer chance that my father read a report of the forthcoming wedding in that sickly society paper Mrs Bellamy drools over.'

'What *are* you going to do now, Serenity? I can't bear your going away on your own. Matron said for you to take leave, then come back here where you belong. She said it was only a nine-days' wonder, and it is, too. Look, Serenity, everyone loved and respected your mother here. She was a wonderful person. She'd been Dr Saveny's receptionist for years and was everyone's trusted friend. She was a counsellor and friend to half the town, and they like you too, so give them a chance. No one will blame you for something that happened before you were born, and they won't condemn her either. Nobody would believe that your mother did anything ugly in her whole life. She'll be remembered for what she was . . . a very special person.'

'No, I won't come back here. I'm not bitter, but I just don't want to live here. I've sold our cottage to the Brent family—I'm so glad I let it out when Mother died. I couldn't have lived there without her, so it was a good thing that I cleared it out and moved into the Nurses' Home, as I couldn't have faced it all now.'

'You'll write to me, Serenity,' Barbie pleaded. 'I don't want to lose touch.'

'Yes, I'll write.'

'Where are you going?'

'Down South. Mother used to talk of the place she grew up in. It was a beautiful valley away in the hills. I'm going to go and have a look. No one will remember her after all these years, and they won't know who I am.'

'Look, I'll take leave and go with you. I've never been down South, either.'

'And leave Robbie? No, I appreciate your offer, but this is something I must do alone. A sort of goodbye present to my mother. Well, I really don't know why I'm going, certainly not to drag up scandal from years back, but who knows what I'll learn.'

She stood up and lifted down the wedding dress. She couldn't mutilate it. And she wasn't going to tell Barbie about the beautiful pressed flower in her mother's bible, nor the photograph wrapped in tissue-paper. She had a feeling that it was her real father and she just wanted to see him, if it was possible. It was a crazy idea, but she had nothing else to do. She was sure he was a nice man, and she had no intention of causing him any embarrassment. He would more than likely be away from there years ago, but it was something to do.

'I'm glad you're taking your wedding dress,' Barbie said. 'You paid for it, it's yours, and I hope that when you find another man you'll invite Robbie and me to the wedding.'

'Have wedding dress, will travel?' Serenity scoffed. 'No, I am not interested in matrimony. Imagine me ever having the nerve to put an engagement in the paper only to find Harvey James appearing out of the blue to inform the future in-laws of my background or lack of it. Only a fool makes the same mistake twice. My mother made a great success of living in no man's land most of her life, I'll do the same.'

'Oh, Serenity, don't think like that. Any man would be proud to have you for a wife. Don't let that awful man ruin your life.'

'Thanks for the vote of confidence, but from my short and rather limited experience of men, I'm not impressed by what they have to offer.'

'Look at Robbie,' Barbie cried. 'He's wonderful.'

Serenity grinned. 'There's always one exception to the rule.'

'How can you still smile?'

'It's better than crying, believe me, I've tried both. Now I've got to be on my way. Are you coming down to the car? You can carry this darned dress. I'd give it to you, but it wouldn't fit.'

Barbie giggled, 'I'm built for comfort not for speed, Robbie says.'

As she took the gown she shrieked. 'You're still wearing John's ring!'

Serenity held out her hand and admired the beautiful ring, turning it so that the magnificent sapphire and tiny diamonds which surrounded it flashed and glowed in the sunlight. 'Quite a rock, isn't it? It cost so much I was frightened to wear it at first. About wearing it, well, John rang from Auckland last night, and he was in such a state with remorse and humiliation at his poor showing, I was sorry for him. He was almost suicidal, and begged me to keep the ring. To calm him down, I said I would for a while. Then he asked would I continue to wear it for at least six months.'

'The nerve . . .' Barbie said angrily.

'Yes, it was rather. He said that all he needed was time and that his mother had blackmailed him into leaving. You know he works for his father and accountants' positions are scarce as hen's teeth, so he said that when he comes back he'll try and get another place, with another firm, and then we could leave this town and be married.'

'He never will, Serenity. Don't trust him. He's absolutely spineless.'

'I know that, but I couldn't tell him, could I? I was scared he might go right off the deep end, as he sounded quite frantic. So I said I'd wear it, and take good care of it for him, but marriage was out for me. It seemed to make him happy, and in six months I'll register it back to him—he'll have got over it by then.'

'And you?'

'I think so.'

'You're a wonderful person, Serenity.'

'I am not,' Serenity replied smartly. 'I have been functioning by remote control most of this week. I hated going back on the wards with everyone knowing that I'd been flunked in my wedding finals. It was like being publicly flogged. I'm still a bit numb, but I have been doing a bit of research, and I'm not a nice person at all. My pride has taken a beating, not my heart, and that's shocking. I can wear John's ring because my love was not very deep, it was more a friendship thing. He is badly hurt because he really loved me.'

'He deserves to be hurt,' Barbie returned savagely.

'No, he does not. I remember when I decided to accept him: he had asked me many times but I didn't feel right about it, then one night I heard Mrs Bellamy on the phone, discussing me with one of her buddies, and she knew I could hear her. She described me as a nice enough girl, a bit nondescript, with no background, no breeding, no money, and mentioned that my mother was only the Doctor's hired help.'

'Oh no!'

'Oh, yes, and what does that make me? I did it to spite her. I knew my mother was worth ten of her, and I thought it would do her the world of good to have to accept me as Mrs Bellamy junior!'

'It would have done John the world of good, too. It might have made a man of him.'

'Not the way you think,' Serenity said. 'I did love him, but I was sorry for him. Sorry for the way she dominated him, and bullied him. He could never call his soul his own. She made his dentist appointments, told him when to shave, chose his clothes; she never let him grow up, and he really was a darling. I would never have pushed him round. I would have helped him to develop his self-confidence and let him be his own person. We could have been happy, but I have to admit that it would have been most satisfying to see him grow strong enough to tell her where to get off. But she won and I lost.'

'No,' Barbie said as they walked to the lift. 'John missed his only chance. I might forgive him, I might even be kind to him when he gets back—he'll need friends—because nobody will admire him for what he did to you that night. What a coward!'

They walked out in the sunshine to the car park. 'Throw that wretched dress in the back seat,' Serenity grimaced. 'I don't know what I'll do with it. And I'd be really grateful if you would be kind to John. He can't help himself, because his mother has so smothered him. Poor John.'

'Poor John,' Barbie echoed. 'He could have had you. But even though you're hurting now, I'm glad you didn't marry him. Robbie and I always knew he wasn't right for you; he was charming, but so weak. You need a strong man to love you, Serenity. You shouldn't agree to marry anyone because you feel sorry for them. That could have been what happened to your mother—you're very like her—then when she met someone she could love deeply, she blew the whole bit. At least you've been saved from that.'

Serenity opened the car door. 'You could be right about Mother, but I doubt it. She was always on about the sanctity of marriage and that loyalty was the greatest thing you could offer your husband. She had very old-fashioned ideas about marriage, she held to the old values, that's why I can't accept that she betrayed her husband. I know that if I had married John, I'd have been faithful to him for my whole life, and as you say, I'm very like her. Something very weird happened but as I'm never likely to find out, then the wise thing to do is not dwell on it. Right, I'm off. And thanks for your support, and your love.'

Barbie grabbed her and hugged her, tears streaming down her face. 'Oh, Serenity, I hate letting you go. You will write? You will be my bridesmaid?'

'That's a promise.' Serenity kissed her, and got into the car. She must not cry. She had loved this town. She had loved John in spite of what she had said to Barbie. Inside she was grieving for him, the way she still grieved for her mother and she was leaving them both behind. And to be losing Barbie too . . . and Robbie. She would have no one to call her own.

'Be happy, Serenity.' Barbie put her hand through the open window.

'Don't go dreaming of a big strong handsome husband for me, Barbie. I don't like handsome men, too conceited, and those strong silent types put me right off altogether. Goodbye, love.'

She moved the car into gear and pressed the accelerator. She was proud that she hadn't cried. She hadn't cried at the cemetery either—some things were too deep for tears. She felt numb and without emotion.

She and her mother were two of a kind—both had messed up their lives in the early stages. Well, her mother had pulled out of it and made something beautiful of her life. Serenity would do the same. But her mother had had a baby to love, and she had nothing to help her start building again. And her mother had had real faith in God, that everything worked together for good, and Serenity didn't even have that to help her. She would just pattern herself on her mother's life and maybe some day it would amount to something. Her mother had lived for others, never wanting much for herself. Perhaps that was the answer.

She put her foot down harder and the car surged forward, heading for Wellington and the ferry. She wondered what the compulsion was to go to the place where her mother was born, and why the urgency to get there. Was it some sort of pilgrimage, that once completed would set her free to start again? Serenity really hoped so. She didn't want to live in this limbo-land of nothingness for too long, she might atrophy, waste away and become seared.

On the third day, Serenity rose early from another sleepless night. She should have taken those sleeping pills Robbie had prescribed for her, but she would tonight. It had been late when she drove into the tiny township, and she had been glad to have a meal and book a room at the one hotel. She walked out in the early morning air and felt refreshed by the cool wind which swept down from the bush-clad hills, bringing the tangy smell of bush with it. There was only a butcher's shop and general store and a few houses that she could see, and the village was perched on the edge of a mighty bluff from which she could glimpse the river glinting through wisps of fog. She had her breakfast and paid her hotel bill, threw her overnight bag in the boot, and got behind the driver's wheel.

She really should have packed the wedding dress in a case. It annoyed her every time she saw it, but it would have taken too much effort to fold it properly. She seemed to have no energy at all, except to drive, and even that wasn't a pleasure. She had not even been aware of the scenery, just miles and miles of native bush, deep gorges, and wild rivers. And now she was heading further inland. What would she do when she got there? Just drive past? . . . or make some excuse and go into the Station, perhaps pretend she was out of petrol? She would think about that later.

The road was winding and narrow, taking Serenity past isolated farms, then native bush again; beautiful as the sun filtered down through the thick leaves and the moss glowed like emerald velvet on the heavy limbs and trunks of the trees.

Heavy morning mist blocked most of her view of the high alps, but she knew they were there. All the way down the South Island they had been on her left-hand side, magnificent and dominating, and now she was driving directly towards them. She was so very tired, and she knew it was foolish to keep driving, but there seemed to be very little traffic on the road. It bothered her, this compulsion to keep driving. The patches of sharp brilliant sunlight, alternating with thin bands of mist, made driving dangerous.

After an hour's driving she left the tar-seal behind and the road wound steeply down to a small bridge, then corkscrewed its way tortuously up another steep grade. The mist was thicker now and Serenity slowed accordingly, straining her eyes to follow the narrow ribbon of road. For a moment the mist cleared. As she put her foot down again she realised she was travelling downhill and far too fast for comfort. Then around the corner only yards from her raced a beautiful deer, bounding and frolicking.

Serenity swung the wheel wide to avoid it, and her wheels spun in the gravel as she skidded violently, barely managing to control the car. She straightened out with a breath of relief and drove round the corner, into a sea of sheep. She stared for one horrid second unable to respond, and the last thing she saw was a man almost over the bonnet of her car as she wrenched the wheel violently and knew she was off the road and somersaulting end over end through trees and fern. She had killed him. She knew it, and Serenity hoped that she would die too. She felt herself free of the car, flying through the air and then . . . nothing.

Serenity opened her eyes slowly then closed them for a long time. The lids seemed so heavy but she tried again, and stared, straight into the face of a man who was gazing at her with such compassion and concern that she knew he wasn't real. He had the kindest face she had ever seen. Perhaps he was an angel come to collect her. She turned her head slightly and knew it must be paradise. She was lying on a soft grassy bank beside a lovely lake and by the edge of the water stood a small deer with a red-jewelled collar, its ears pricked forward, watching her with enormous eyes, and by its feet lay two dogs. Dogs and deer did not play together, not on earth they didn't. Then the mist in the centre of the lake swirled and lifted, rolling in threads and spirals into the sunlight, and she looked right across the lake and beyond to the most glorious valley she had ever seen.

The luxuriant grass-clad slopes rose gently upwards towards dark purple bush-clad hills, and higher yet to snow-clad peaks. At the edge of the bush on a plateau surrounded by a sheltering of trees was a white homestead shining pure white in the morning sun, and the windows shone pure gold.

Serenity turned back to examine the man who knelt in front of her, his warm hazel eyes watching her. The odd feeling of weightlessness took over again as if she was floating above the earth. She had seen him before, and as the sun struck sharply on the strong planes of his face, she remembered the man in front of her car. So she had killed him, and he was here waiting with her in the wonderful place.

'I'm sorry. I didn't mean to kill you.'

He smiled and deep smile lines grooved each side of his cheeks.

'You missed, but it was a fairly determined effort.' His voice was deep and pleasant.

Carefully she put out her hand and touched his tanned face, feeling it firm and hard under her fingers. 'You're sure?'

'Absolutely. Although I hope heaven looks a bit like this. Now, how do you feel?'

'I fell beautiful, woozy and warm and . . . nothing.'

'No pain at all?'

'No.'

'I'll just check for broken bones then I'll carry you up to the Land-Rover.'

She felt his hands move over her body, firm and impersonal, but with skill. 'Nothing broken and no bleeding. How lucky can you get?'

'My car?'

'Not so lucky, I'm afraid—it's a write-off. You could not have had your seatbelt on. Most reprehensible, but this time it saved your life because you must have been flung out on the way down.'

'I forgot. I wasn't thinking straight.'

The man's well-defined lips curved into another smile. 'You weren't driving straight either. If you had been I would have been flattened. Thanks for dodging me even if you risked your own neck to do it. What is your name?'

'Serenity James.'

'My, that does suit you. Mine is Hudson Grey. Take my hand and see if you can stand.'

Serenity took his hand and pulled herself to her feet, then her knees shook so badly she clung to him to save herself from falling. 'I'm sorry about this . . .'

Again his smile charmed her. Those deep attractive grooves showed he must smile often. 'I'll carry you.'

She found herself lifted effortlessly and slipped her arm about his neck to balance herself. 'It's all uphill. Can you make it?'

He laughed, 'You're as light as a feather.' He whistled the dogs and they rushed past with the small deer in hot pursuit.

Snuggled safely against his tartan bush-shirt, she felt more secure than she could ever remember, like a baby being comforted. 'Is that a tame deer?'

'Yes, that's Bambi. Not an original name, but it suits him. My housekeeper raised him, and now he won't stay at home. I've put a collar on him studded with reflectors so that he won't get shot by mistake.'

He paused by a large fallen tree. 'You sit here while I catch my breath, then tell me what you'll want from your car.'

He lowered her to her feet, and she said, 'I told you I was heavy. I'm thin but I'm fairly tall.'

'Heart-high,' he offered with a grin.

She smiled shakily, but he was right, so he must be very tall himself. 'Oh, look at my car! What a mess!'

'Are you insured?'

'Yes, I am.'

'Then don't worry about it. If you'd been inside, it would have been curtains, I'm afraid. I think I'd better take everything. We don't have much thieving out this way, but you can never tell.'

She watched him leap over the broken trees and quickly retrieve her cases from the boot which was comparatively free from damage. Then he leaned into the car and lifted out her overnight bag and her wedding gown in its plastic cover, and came back to her.

'I'm afraid anything in the front is worthless. It's more like kindling wood there. Was there anything of special value?'

'No, only road maps and a book I was reading . . . and my purse. I should like that.'

'I've got that—it must have been thrown over the back. Getting married soon?' He held the dress up.

'No. I don't know. That's funny, I can't remember anything about it. Why I'm carrying it . . .'

'Don't worry, it'll all come back. You've had a pretty bad shake-up, probably temporary amnesia, and therefore I'd like to get you home as soon as possible. I've left my sheep on the road and I don't want anyone else ploughing into them. Some clot left my road gate open last night and I lost the lot.'

Serenity made an attempt to stand but her knees buckled and she collapsed back on the log.

'Just sit there,' Hudson said sharply. 'I'll take this stuff up to the Land-Rover and be right back.'

She watched him stride easily up the steep bank carrying her two heavy cases as if they were empty, and her wedding dress draped incongruously over his broad back only seemed to emphasise the sheer physical strength of the man. She felt a tinge of resentment at his peremptory order to sit quiet and wait, as if he was used to giving orders and equally used to having them obeyed, then knew that she was being ridiculous because she had no choice in the matter.

'Ready now?'

She looked up surprised at Hudson Grey's swift return and was again struck by the essential good humour and kindness in his expressive grey-green eyes.

'Sorry to be such a nuisance.'

His grin widened showing strong even white teeth, 'I wouldn't describe you that way, Serenity.'

As he scooped her up in his arms, she again felt incredibly secure and protected and something else . . . strangely exhilarated, as if some of his magnificent vitality was being transferred to her. She was disgusted at herself. She was actually enjoying being treated as a weak and helpless female and that was entirely contrary to her nature. She had always avoided strong, domineering men and yet here she was lapping up this new sensation and finding it exceedingly pleasant. It must be the result of the accident, concussion probably.

Hudson eased her gently on to the wide leather seat of his Land-Rover and closed the door before striding round to the driver's seat.

'Here's a can of soft drink. Sorry I haven't anything stronger to offer at the moment. It will only take a few minutes to get these sheep in the gate; and then I'll take you home.'

Serenity ripped off the tab and thankfully swallowed the lukewarm drink. She didn't feel faint, but her mouth was dry and nervous and her body was quivering with unexpected vibrations. It was as if all the tension and worry of the past weeks and the sleepless nights and compulsive driving towards this valley had caught up on her. She felt simultaneously drained of energy and listless, yet bubbling with an excitement that was beyond her control.

Almost objectively she watched Hudson Grey concentrate on his work, driving the vehicle up to the

stragglers of the mob of sheep, whistling and command-
ing his dogs and thumping the side of the door to urge the
sheep faster. He seemed entirely absorbed, his whole
concentration riveted on the job, then he unexpectedly
flashed a quick glance at her.

'You okay?'

'Certainly,' Serenity replied a little primly.

'Great.' His smile was full of charm and he turned
back to the droving.

As the last sheep crossed the wide wooden bridge
which spanned a deep brown stream at the entrance
gate, Hudson called in his dogs and drove across, then
braked and went back to shut the gate.

She turned in her seat to watch him swing the gate to,
and with the same ease and economy of movement that
marked his every action, he fastened the chain, strode
back to the Land-Rover, and slipped into his place. The
sunlight glinted on his thick auburn hair and again
highlighted the unusual planes of his face and strong
jawline. He was an exceedingly attractive man and
Serenity was appalled to find his very presence beside
her was the cause of the excitement she had noted
previously.

She closed her eyes and leaned back against the seat
and took several deep breaths.

'Are you in pain, Serenity?' Hudson demanded, concern obvious in his voice.

At the touch of his hand on her shoulder her grey eyes
flew open and she smiled at him for the first time. 'No.
Confused maybe, and a little shocked, but definitely no
pain.'

His intelligent eyes scrutinised her for another
moment before being assured of the truth of her statement, then, lightly flicking her cheek with his hand, he
eased the Land-Rover forward. 'The sooner I get you

home the better. You'd spoil a good bath.'

It was only then that she became aware of her torn dress and laddered stockings and the fact that she was well bedaubed with mud and one shoe was missing.

'I'm a real mess,' she stated but without concern.

'What's a bit of mud? You've had a fantastically lucky escape. When I think of your car with the engine pushed in on the front seat . . . ! And we're eighty miles from a hospital here.'

Yes, she had escaped death by inches and that would account for this sense of peace and happiness that filled her being. Or was that something to do with Hudson Grey himself? She knew that the warmth of his smile and the deep tones in his voice had melted something hidden within herself and it triggered little alarm bells of apprehension. Serenity became aware that he was whistling a gay lilting tune that matched her mood. She was sure she knew the tune but could not think of the words.

She leaned over then touched his arm to get his attention, her attractive face bright with interest, 'What *are* you whistling? It's so familiar yet I can't place it.'

He grinned, 'It's very appropriate. Listen.' And in a smooth and pleasant baritone began to sing.

> '*Early one morning, just as the sun was rising,*
> *I heard a maiden singing in the valley below.*'

'Of course,' Serenity laughed and joined in with him to finish it.

> '*Oh don't deceive me. Oh, never leave me.*
> *How could you use a poor maiden so?*'

'I haven't sung that since I was in school,' Hudson said. 'It just flashed into my mind. You weren't exactly singing, but you were in the valley below, and just as the sun was rising. But I can assure you I have no intention of deceiving you, nor of holding you prisoner. You may leave when you wish.'

'Thank you. It was a school song of mine, too, but I can only remember a part of the next verse.

'Oh, gay are the garlands and red are the roses,
I culled from the garden to bind on my brow.

'Yes, that's it, very sad and romantic, but a pretty tune. I don't often have adventures, especially not romantic ones, and I plan to enjoy this one.'

His smile was full of charm and Serenity found his buoyant good humour highly contagious and smiled in return. Not that she wanted any romance or adventure, she had had enough drama to satisfy her for a lifetime.

CHAPTER TWO

SERENITY was feeling slightly breathless as the Land-Rover swept in a wide circle and stopped in front of a large attractive white homestead which she had sighted through the morning mist across the lake.

'I thought the windows were made of pure gold, it looked so very beautiful.'

'I know. It's the way it's situated on this plateau and the first rays of the rising sun have that effect. Now, let's be having you.'

'I'm sure I can walk. You can't carry me everywhere.'

'Rubbish.' He picked her up almost carelessly and strode along the cement path and into a modern-styled kitchen and down a step into a large comfortably furnished lounge, then placed her on a sofa.

'Sit there while I get you a stiff brandy.'

'I really don't need a stimulant,' she protested.

As if she hadn't spoken he moved to a drinks cabinet and poured out two generous measures and returned. 'Here's yours. Drink it and don't argue. You may not need it but I do. You're not the only one who's lucky to be alive this morning. You didn't miss me by all that much.'

Shaken by the remembrance of how close she had been to him, she downed her drink and grimaced.

'Not your favourite tipple?' he asked with an amused grin. 'Never mind, it will do you good. Now I'll run you a bath.'

'I'm quite capable of running my own bath if you'll show me the bathroom,' Serenity said, but was annoyed to find herself talking to thin air. Hudson had already disappeared through another door and soon she heard the sound of running water. He really was a hard man to argue with, or should she say an impossible man?

Then, as the effect of the brandy hit her, she felt warmed and relaxed and looked about her, appreciating the pleasant proportions of the lounge and the magnificent view of the valley from the floor-to-ceiling windows. Off the kitchen and on a slightly higher level she could see a dining room with a large oval table, and a floor of polished wood. The whole atmosphere was attractive, spacious and airy, welcoming and comfortable. She liked the massive fireplace and stone surround, and the massive *kauri* mantelpiece that ran the full width of the far wall. A wonderful stag's head with upswept antlers was on one wall and silver cups and family photographs on the mantelpiece, then behind her she heard a soft whirring sound and looked to see two huge native pigeons alight on a flowering tree almost within hand's reach from the window.

What a wonderful place to live. Then she saw Hudson crossing the patio carrying her cases, and he was still whistling his song. She giggled a little. He was still enjoying his romantic adventure.

'Which case do you want open?' He deposited them in front of her. 'I'll put your purse and wedding gown in your room while you fish out some clean gear.'

As he spoke, her purse catapulted open and the contents flew over the floor. 'Sorry about that. I noticed the catch was broken when I took it from the car and I was being careful.'

He knelt and quickly replaced her things, then held the photo of John up for closer inspection. 'Is this the lucky guy?'

'I suppose so,' Serenity muttered.

'You suppose so! Don't you know? You're wearing his ring, aren't you?' He gave her a sharp glance.

'Yes, I'm wearing his ring, but whether he's lucky or not is a matter for conjecture,' she said with considerable asperity.

He turned the photo over and to her annoyance read out loud John's silly verse.

> Serenity James is tall and slim,
> Serenity James has an enchanting grin,
> Serenity James has a figure divine,
> And Serenity James is mine . . . all mine.

Well, he seems pretty sure he's got it made, quite boastful in fact.'

Serenity stared out the window. Yes, John had been so boastful about their engagement, about her loving him . . .

'Hey, you're not still having trouble remembering, are you?' Hudson was all concern. He stuffed the photo back in the purse. 'I'm an idiot.'

'No. It's okay. Everything's coming back now.' The trouble was that she had been gloriously free of regrets and resentments for the past hour, and she didn't want it all coming back. She had actually been enjoying herself, laughing, even singing.

'I've made you cry, I'm sorry. You're probably more shaken up than you realise. I've got to get you into a bath then into bed, and then you can ring this chap up and tell him you're safe and well. Which case do you want opened?'

Serenity pointed to the smaller case, and Hudson flicked the latches open and pulled it closer to her before picking up the other case, together with her purse and dress and headed off through the far door.

She leaned forward, angry at herself for the tears which had fallen so unexpectedly. She scrubbed them away from her eyes, then lifted out her toilet bag, some clean undies, a pair of jeans and sneakers and a pretty blue scooped-necked top. She loved this top with its heavy embossed satin butterflies. She had chosen it to wear on her honeymoon.

'Got everything?' Hudson asked cheerfully. 'The bath is run, and I've put out the towels.'

He bent down and lifted her back into his arms, then, balancing her on his knee, piled her things into her arms and strode for the far door.

'This is unnecessary,' Serenity cried angrily. 'Put me down.'

Ignoring her he carried her up a short flight of stairs, elbowed the bathroom door open, and deposited her on a chair beside a hot bath. 'Do you think you can manage by yourself?'

'And what do you propose to offer if I can't?' Serenity asked in quelling tones.

'Well, sing out if you feel faint or anything.'

'I will not faint or anything,' she informed him firmly.

'No, I'm sure you won't. You just don't look the fainting sort. Pity. I'll be in the kitchen making a cup of tea. Your bedroom is directly opposite. Take as long as you like then hop into bed and I'll bring you up a cuppa.'

'I *won't* go to bed. I'll come down for my tea, thank you.'

She heard him whistling again as he went downstairs. She looked about her with appreciation at the well-appointed bathroom. This Hudson Grey didn't stint himself when it came to comfort. She stripped and eased her stiff achy body into the hot bath, then sniffed inelegantly. He must have added the fragrant bath oil with a liberal hand. She didn't know what he had used but she would bet it was expensive. It was absolutely divine, and Serenity felt lapped in luxury.

As she soaked in the hot water she relaxed completely, the combination of the heavenly perfume and the glass of brandy brought a sense of euphoria and she idly speculated on Hudson Grey and his life-style. This bathroom, for instance, was definitely feminine. It certainly wasn't *his* bathroom, no sign of a razor or masculine talc or after-shave. Who used it? His wife . . . no, he said he had a housekeeper, not that having a housekeeper precluded having a wife, but somehow he didn't seem married. There was something free and untamed in his attitude that did not speak of running in double harness . . . an arrogance, a certain stance.

Still, she felt sure there was a woman in his life . . . or women. He was too much at ease with her to be one of those embittered and dedicated bachelor types. Whoever the woman was, Serenity did not envy her. As she had told Barbie, the dominating male had never appealed to her, and Hudson Grey was definitely bossy and absolutely dedicated to having his own way.

However, he had been good to her. It would have been horrible to come out of that crash with no one around and to have waited ages on that lonely road for someone to drive by. Gosh, she was muddled in her thinking. If Hudson Grey and his deer, dogs and sheep had not been in that exact spot she would not have crashed.

She hooked the chain with her toe and as the water drained away she dried herself in a large soft pink towel, then wrapped it about her sarong fashion and washed her hair under the shower before dressing leisurely. She was in no hurry to cross swords with her host. What a ridiculous thought! There was no earthly reason for feeling that they would be antagonists. She merely had to thank him for his hospitality, arrange with some garage to retrieve her car, and arrange transport for herself to the nearest town . . . that would be Greymouth. He said the car was a write-off, so maybe the insurance company might just view it where it was.

She glanced in the mirror at her boy-slim figure and took satisfaction from the neat cut of her jeans and the smooth fit of her top. She ran her comb once more through her wet fair hair. That brilliant sunshine would soon dry it, silky and shining. It would turn under at the ends naturally, a style which suited her pale oval face and wide grey eyes. Bracing herself, she picked up her discarded clothes and crossed to the bedroom to drop them on top of her suitcase. This room, like the rest of the house, was charming, restful and inviting and the view across to the Southern Alps was fabulous.

'Are you going to be all day?'

Serenity frowned. Hudson must have heard her leave the bathroom . . . what an impatient beast he was. She took her time going down the stairs, and found him crossing the dining room carrying a large tray with cakes, scones and teapot, milk, sugar and cups.

'Hurry up. We'll have it on the patio. You look as if a bit of good West Coast sunshine would not go amiss.'

Resentfully, Serenity followed him. No girl appreciated being told she was pale and wan. It was mainly tiredness and stress anyway. 'What's the great rush? You told me to take my time.'

He answered with a cheerful grin, 'I've just taken these hot scones from the oven and wanted you to enjoy them. Hot buttered scones and raspberry jam are irresistible. Milk? Sugar?'

Serenity eased into a wrought-iron chair and narrowed her eyes. '*You* cooked them?'

'Such cynicism in one so young. It's painful. Milk? Sugar?'

'Milk, no sugar, thank you.' She noted he had removed his red tartan shirt, and his athletic frame looked even more vital in jeans and loose-knit short-sleeved shirt. 'You don't look the sort to be messing around in the kitchen.'

His tanned face creased into an even deeper smile as he passed her a cup of piping hot tea. 'I didn't say I'd cooked them, I said I'd just taken them from the oven. My housekeeper, who spoils me utterly, knew my weakness and baked a raft full of them before she left. She put them in the deep freeze, and I just had to heat them. You do jump to conclusions, I must remember that . . . try one.'

She took a scone and bit into it thoughtfully. Yes, he was just the kind of man a housekeeper would spoil, or any woman actually, and he had meant her to misunderstand. She felt annoyed, then felt annoyed that she was annoyed. She didn't usually let people irritate her.

'Feeling better? Are you sure you shouldn't have a lie down?'

'Positive, and I'm fine, thank you,' Serenity answered calmly. He wouldn't be above picking her up and flinging her into bed if he thought she needed it.

'Good. As soon as you finish this, you must go and ring your fiancé, then your insurance company. I'm sure there's one locally, as they have branches throughout New Zealand. But John must be told first, he's first on the agenda. I bet he'll be a bit shaken to know he nearly lost you.'

'I can't reach him, he's overseas.'

'For how long? When's the wedding?'

Serenity drew a deep breath. It felt like a third degree; that blasted wedding dress, she should have snipped it to pieces, then she wouldn't feel such a fool. 'He'll be back in six to eight weeks.'

'So why are you carrying your wedding dress with you?' He took another scone and bit into it with relish, his hazel eyes watching her with bright curiosity.

'Mind your own damned business!' Serenity was appalled to hear herself shout. She rarely swore, it showed a certain lack of vocabulary, but he infuriated her. Still, he *had* been kind. 'I was to have been married last week, then John had to leave unexpectedly. I had already given my notice, so I just threw everything in the car and here I am. Sorry to bite your head off. I'm just a bit touchy on the subject.'

'That's understandable. Have another scone. You haven't quarrelled or anything? He still wants to marry you, does he?'

'Oh yes, he still wants to marry me,' Serenity told him gravely, glad he had not worded the question towards her attitude about the wedding.

'That's okay then. Why didn't he take you with him? He's a bit of a fool in my opinion, leaving a pretty girl like you hanging about.'

Serenity felt her colour rise at the compliment. 'We *did* consider it, but the firm wasn't at all keen.'

'So you're at a loose end for a month or so; that's very interesting. What are you doing in this part of the world?'

Carefully avoiding the last part of his question, she demanded, 'What's interesting about me having nothing to do for two months?'

'Well, as I told you, my housekeeper has left, and I need someone to take over. I prefer not to employ someone long term. I might be getting married myself . . . so it would suit me to have an interim arrangement until I make up my mind.'

'And you're offering me the job?' Serenity's grey eyes opened wide in surprise. 'You don't even know that I can cook. I can positively assure you that I would *not* spoil you.'

He threw back his head and laughed. 'I wouldn't expect you to, my dear girl. Just cooking and cleaning, and if you care for it, a bit of outside work. Do you like riding?'

'Oh,' she drew a deep breath, 'that would be wonderful. I love riding.' Then added quickly. 'That doesn't mean I'm accepting the position.'

'Of course not, but it helps. Are you a good rider?'

'No. But I love horses. I had my own pony when I was a kid, and I ride whenever I get the chance. I belonged to a pony club for a while, but Ebony hated going over the jumps, and I wasn't competition minded. I just like riding for my own pleasure.'

'Well, we've got plenty of horses here, and if none of them suits you, I might take you out on the riverbed and you can choose your own. My father loves horses too. He put some Arab mares out there, and we've still got about ten or fifteen careering up and down the river. You can take your pick. I've a friend who is breaking them in and selling them in his spare time. He'll train it for you.'

Serenity closed her eyes, and as if in a dream saw a mob of wild horses galloping through the bush, and plunging in and out of the river, the spray flying and their manes and tails streaming in the wind. And she could have any one she chose.

'You didn't say what you're doing in this part of the world?'

Talk about single-minded! But she determined she was not going to let him worry at her like a dog with a bone. 'That's private business.' She kept her eyes shut so that he could not read the expression in her eyes.

'How long have you lived in this area, Hudson?' She was searching for clues and if he was just a new-comer she would not waste her time on him.

'All my life. Born here, well almost. My mother said with Dad's careless regard for time it was lucky they made it to the Maternity Hospital in time. But it was different in those days. For instance, there were no roads in, just tracks across the paddocks, fords instead of bridges and culverts, real pioneering stuff.'

Keeping her eyes closed she ran her fingers through her hair, feeling the tiny curls about her face already springing back into place. She could *feel* him staring at her intently.

'Want another cup of tea?'

'No, thanks.'

'Well, I do,' he said cheerfully, then as if sensing her interest he continued, 'When I say I was born here, I don't mean on this side of the river. We only bought this about five years ago, so we own the whole valley now, something my father always dreamed about, when he came here as a young man.'

Serenity opened her eyes and gazed at the lush green pastures and well fenced paddocks, the silver ribbon of river which flashed between the native bush and to her left the perfection of the lake, and feasted her eyes on the great purple-green forest-clad hills which encircled the valley and beyond them the Southern Alps in all their glory.

'Beautiful, just beautiful . . . any man would dream of owning this.'

'Yes, you're right. We've been very fortunate, but dreams don't just happen, they have to be worked at. When he came here there were no roads, no power, no telephone, no fences; it was really wild country, just a run.'

'It's still wild and rugged looking, lonely and lovely.'

'You'd get on with my father. He just loves the Haupiri as much today as when he first discovered it; it's part of him and he's part of it . . . my mother, too, of course. She was a city girl, and it must have been tough on her adapting to the isolation and the hardships, in the beginning. The Bar 2 would never have been the success it is today if she had not been the woman she is . . . you need a strong and intelligent mate beside you to subdue this kind of country.'

The love and admiration for his parents was deep and Serenity was oddly affected by his openness in speaking of it. To cover the emotion she felt, she asked quickly, 'Why do you call it the Bar 2?'

'That's the brand, a bar with a 2 under it. It's the name of the Station. The cattle and horses and saddles were all branded with the 2 when my father came here, and he liked the idea and so registered it—but today only the wool goes out that way.'

It was obvious that he enjoyed talking about the Station, and she watched him as she listened to his deep attractive voice describing the early days and the trials and triumphs. She hardly noticed the time passing as he spoke of his own childhood and his years at boarding school, and at Lincoln Agricultural College, his year in Canada and a further year in Europe and Scandinavia.

Abruptly he stopped. 'I must have bored you stupid. Why didn't you stop me?'

'No,' she protested. 'I've loved listening. It's just so unexpected, away out here in the backblocks. After travelling all those miles through bush and swamps I didn't expect to find a wide fertile valley hidden in the hills, and you . . . sitting there at ease talking of painting, literature, European history and architecture. It's a surprise, that's all.'

'In what way?' He sounded faintly amused.

'Well, I would have expected to find people living a fairly uncouth, hill-billy style of life here in this isolation.' As soon as she said it she coloured with embarrassment—it sounded so appallingly rude. She had been thinking it but should never have spoken it out so baldly.

With a dead-pan expression he replied, 'Oh, I'm very definitely couth, and my parents are even more so.'

She giggled and then laughed outright. It sounded so ridiculous.

He joined in. 'I'll make allowances for the knock you've had on your head. You should laugh more often.'

'Why?' she demanded in surprise.

'The change is quite dramatic.'

'In what way?'

'I've been watching you as you listened. With that fair hair and delicate oval face plus the wide-eyed incredibly innocent expression, I thought you looked like a little old-fashioned Quaker girl, pure as driven snow, and . . .'

'And?' she echoed aggressively.

'And then you laughed, and you became all Eve, warm, soft, and seductive. It's quite intriguing. I must make you laugh more often.'

'I won't be here long enough to allow you to indulge in your fantasies,' she said crushingly.

He laughed. 'It must be the name, I think. Serenity. Are you calm, serene and gentle, an unflappable girl?'

'I used to be,' Serenity admitted.

'Before this wedding mix-up, you mean.'

'No. Before that, when my mother was alive. Our life was pleasant, peaceful and I suppose you could say predictable. Since I lost her . . .' she sighed.

'Has that happened fairly recently?' he asked sympathetically.

'About eighteen months ago.' She blinked hard as she felt the tears forming in her eyes. Why was she being so honest with this man? Why was the pain coming back today? Was it because she was aware that somewhere close to this place her mother had grown up? 'Oh, look here's your pet deer.'

She was glad of an excuse to change the subject and watched fascinated as Bambi trotted delicately up the rise on slender legs, then with a disdainful glance at the closed gate bounded lightly over the fence and walked up to them.

Hudson leaned forward and fed Bambi a scone, but when Bambi wanted another he pushed him away. 'Get off. You'll get fat.'

'You're just greedy,' Serenity commented. 'You're keeping the scones for yourself. I'm going to give him one.'

'Go ahead,' he encouraged her with a smile. 'When he finds you're a soft touch you'll never get any peace. Are you going to take my offer of a job?'

'I might.'

'You do move cautiously. I'll have to bait the hook a bit more attractively. What will it take?'

'Probably more than you have to offer,' Serenity replied with an edge in her voice . . . he really did have a colossal conceit.

He grinned unrepentantly. 'Oh, I have a lot to offer, I haven't started yet . . . well, only the horse.'

Turning her gaze from his wickedly teasing hazel eyes she felt her colour rise, but concentrated on the fabulous view until she could ask in a casual tone, 'Have you many neighbours?'

'Do you think you'd get lonely? Oh, I'd see to it that you didn't.'

Hearing the laughter in his voice she glared at him. 'You have an inflated opinion of your own appeal. I *prefer* solitude. The reason I asked about neighbours was that I nursed someone from here once and I wondered if the people mentioned still lived here.'

'What was her name?'

'I didn't say what sex my patient was, and I would consider it a breach of confidence to discuss any of the circumstances with you. Perhaps if you offered me a few names I would recognise the one I'm looking for.'

'Well, if they were in the farming line there are only a few to offer. Most of the holdings out here are quite large, and there would be all told only half a dozen owners.' He rattled off several names.

Serenity shook her head. 'No, they don't sound familiar. Perhaps they have sold out and left years ago.'

Hudson frowned. 'If you would be a little more specific, I could probably help you. These places tend to stay in the family, but off hand I can think of only one that has changed several times in the past twenty years, that's Seaforths. Taylor's had it before them, and Rotheram's before that . . . Twenty years ago there was a thriving mill below the Haupiri bridge. People came and went all the time, but when they were here they really identified with the district. Then there have always been farm workers and contractors, temporary people, too many for me to remember off-hand.'

Serenity felt her hopes sliding away. She wasn't going to find any trace of her mother. Perhaps her grandparents had left immediately after the scandal, if there had been a scandal. She knew so little. Maybe they had only been farm workers and moving about a lot, but that had not been her impression.

Hudson sat in thoughtful silence, then said in a genuinely puzzled voice, 'Sorry, I can't help you. Are you sure you've got the right area? Remember you're on the West Coast now. It's a close-knit community; friends, relatives can live miles away from each other and can still describe themselves as neighbours or near-by. Bell Hill Plains has been brought into production recently, and Rotomanu Valley has a big farming community and they are definitely our neighbours. Years ago all our cattle were driven out to the railhead at Rotomanu. Look, I'll get you the phone book and you can run your fingers down the names. Perhaps you'll come up with something.'

'Forget it. It wasn't that important.' Serenity tried to make her remark in a light voice, but she was terribly depressed. She had not realised just how important the end of the journey had become to her, not until this very minute.

'If my father were here, I'm sure he could help you. He's got a phenomenal memory. He can recall everyone who has ever worked here, in fact he can remember anyone who has been in the Haupiri, but he and mother are overseas for a few months.'

'I said not to worry about it.' Serenity got out of her chair and walked over to stroke Bambi.

'It couldn't be the Tarrants . . . Old Tom and Sarah Tarrant. They've never been out of this valley so you couldn't have nursed them. I know that for a fact. They died within a week of each other five years ago. I bought this place off them. Well, off Sarah! Old Tom was a right old tyrant, but Sarah and I were mates.'

Serenity's hand froze on the sleek slender neck, making Bambi flinch nervously. With iron control she concluded the stroke downward and sat back on her heels fixing her gaze fiercely on the highest mountain peak, gratitude welling up in her that she was not facing Hudson right at this moment. Her mother had lived *here*.

'I suppose she spoiled you too, this Sarah.' Serenity ventured in a flat and hopefully disinterested tone.

'Ah, Sarah Tarrant was different, a truly wonderful woman, a real lady. Yes, I was a favourite of hers. Now *she* did live a hard life, and being married to Old Tom didn't make it any easier. He was a hard unforgiving chap, twisted and bitter, and the meaner he got the more loving and gentle she became. He fought with everyone, she loved everyone . . .'

'Including him?' The question came a bit thickly.

'Oh, most definitely including him, and he did nothing to deserve that love. He was so cantankerous, so mean-spirited that I often felt like laying one on him to teach him to treat her better, yet she wouldn't have thanked me for it. She never answered him back, didn't even seem to notice his rudeness. She loved him and that love had a curious quality to it, a warmth, a depth that was beyond the ordinary.'

'You sound envious,' Serenity was careful not to turn towards him.

'Any man would be, they don't make them that way today. She was beautiful, even in her eighties. She was loving, absolutely loyal, even submissive, yet no door-mat. She was highly educated, and had charm and a rare dignity. Sarah Tarrant was very special, to me, and to the whole district.'

Serenity stealthily slid her hand into her pocket and pulled out her handkerchief to wipe away the silent tears which slid down her face. She didn't want him to know she was crying . . . crying for a grandmother whom he had known and loved and whom she would never meet. She made up her mind. She was going to take his job, no matter what it cost her, because she wanted to stay here and learn more about Sarah Tarrant, but she wouldn't tell him yet. He must not connect her decision with this conversation.

'You must have met someone fairly special yourself if you are contemplating marriage.' She marvelled at her own composure.

He laughed without humour and abruptly got to his feet. 'There will be no love in the marriage I'm considering, mutual respect but not love.'

Serenity walked forward to help him clear the table. 'Don't be silly. You must love her or you couldn't possibly think of spending a lifetime with her.'

'Indeed I can think of it. In fact love is the one ingredient I do not want in my marriage.'

Serenity picked up her cup and saucer, then put it down in the same spot. He wasn't fooling, he was serious. She felt absurdly shaken and gazed at him with shocked grey eyes. 'Why not? Why not love?'

'Been there, done that, next question.' His voice was harsh.

'Don't be flippant. What do you mean? That you've been in love and it didn't work out. Perhaps she wasn't the right girl.'

'Oh, yes, she was the right girl. I built this house for her. Don't you think it's a nice house?'

'Yes, yes I do,' Serenity said, a little uncertainly. There was something here that she was missing. In a flash, Hudson had changed from the pleasant, if annoying, smiling conversationalist to a granite man with a hard expression and challenging cynical eyes.

'Glad you like it.' He picked up the tray and walked through to the kitchen. 'The phone is through there, or if you prefer more privacy, use my office; it's at the head of the stairs.'

'I'm only ringing the insurance company,' Serenity said slowly. 'Why didn't you marry her, if she was the right girl?'

'She died,' he replied flatly. 'Do you want me to find the number for you?'

'No, thank you.' Serenity hurried through the door and took a deep breath. Whew! Her hand was shaking as she searched for the number. How could she ever have thought he was kind? His voice might have been without emotion, but anger flared in his eyes as if . . . as if he *blamed* the poor girl for dying. As if he *hated* her for spoiling his plans.

When Serenity returned to the kitchen, she found him wiping the bench. 'I could have rinsed those through.'

'Oh, I'm housetrained; the minor problems of fending for myself don't trouble me. Don't take the job out of a mistaken idea that I need rescuing. I don't need anyone to feel sorry for me. No woman is indispensable in my life. Remember that if you do decide to stay.'

'I don't feel in the least sorry for you,' Serenity said sharply.

'That's good.' He laughed, his good humour suddenly restored. 'Tell you what, we'll make a bargain. I won't make a pass at you if you promise you won't make a pass at me.'

Her grey eyes flashed. 'I'll give it to you in writing if you like. What makes you think you're irresistible?'

'Oh, I've had my offers.' His hazel eyes were lit with laughter. 'If you had fended off as many eager females as I have, you'd be wary too. I've got a lot to offer. I'm well-heeled, come from an impeccable background, and with due modesty I think I'm reasonably attractive.'

She knew he was teasing her, but couldn't resist saying tartly, 'Not to me, you're not.'

He roared laughing. 'Such devastating honesty. I find you completely fascinating.'

'And I find you completely infuriating,' she flung at him.

'That could change. Come on, we'll ride out to the river and see the horses. Every woman has her price.'

Tight-lipped, she followed him out the back door and across to the stables. She wanted to yell at him to keep his rotten horse, but as she climbed on the yard rail and watched him catch and saddle the horses, she knew she wasn't going to do that. He was right that everyone had a price, and he didn't know that he had already offered hers. She relaxed as she regained her composure, and could even smile as he came towards her leading the horses. He thought he was so smart, yet he didn't know she had already made up her mind to stay on the Bar 2. Her mother had lived here, and her grandparents, and Hudson had said these stations rarely changed hands, so maybe she would meet the man whose faded photograph was wrapped in fine tissue-paper.

As she slid down to the ground, he handed her the reins. 'Hold these a minute.'

She stroked the fine arched neck of the smaller horse. 'I hope you're mine, you lovely thing.'

'Yes, I'll give you Misty; you need a quiet mount if you haven't ridden for a while.'

'Thanks. What a fabulous saddle.' She examined the intricate carving.

'A real Mexican saddle. My father brought it home when I was a teenager. Thought you might appreciate it; it's as comfortable as a rocking chair to sit on. Here, you'd better wear this, otherwise you'll be burnt to a crisp.'

She turned towards him, still holding the horses, and he put a white cowboy hat on her fair hair and pulled the cord to fit snugly under her chin. 'White for purity,' he commented with a grin.

'Thank you.'

'For the hat, or the remark?' Suddenly serious, he dropped his hands lightly on to her shoulders. 'You do love this John of yours, don't you, Serenity?'

Annoyed, she felt herself colour. 'Yes, I do, I told you that.'

'Good.' His eyes held hers with an unnerving scrutiny. 'I wouldn't have you here otherwise. I don't want complications in my life.'

'I can't answer for you, but I promise you, you'll never be a complication in my life,' she said crushingly.

He grinned and flung an arm across her shoulders, giving her a hug. 'I have a feeling we're going to be good friends, Serenity. I find it a stimulating thought. I can tease you, flirt with you if I want to, and all with perfect immunity . . .'

'Take your hands off me. I don't believe in body-contact sports.'

He smiled wickedly as he took the reins of his horse from her. 'You don't think that was a pass, I hope. Little lady, when I make a pass at you, you'll be in no danger of not knowing what I'm doing.'

Ignoring him, Serenity gathered in her reins, slipped her foot into the stirrup, and mounted in one fluid movement. He was right, the saddle was the epitome of comfort.

'Nice. Come on, then.'

She confidently kicked Misty into a trot and followed him down the gravel road past the sheepyards. It was bliss to be back on a horse, and she would have felt completely happy if she had not had a sneaking suspicion that she was doing a crazy thing by accepting this offer of employment. Hudson Grey disconcerted her. He was all the things she disliked in a man, suave, sophisticated, and full of self-confidence, well . . . arrogantly sure of himself, really. If that's all there was to him, she could handle that, but she could not deny that he was exceedingly attractive, that he had masculine magnetism that disturbed her, and there was that hardness in him that almost amounted to leashed violence. Swiftly she altered her decision. She would not stay here. As soon as the insurance agent checked her car, she would leave.

'What do you think of it?' Hudson had reined in and was watching her carefully.

'What do I think of what?' Serenity was annoyed that she had been so deep in thought that she had become unaware of her surroundings.

'Sarah Tarrant's house. I thought you might like to see it.'

Serenity looked towards the old rambling, unpainted house, its timbers weathered silver by time, its roof red-brown with rust. Roses and honeysuckle climbed the railings of the broad verandah which encircled the house, and she loved it. The garden was a riot of flowers, roses and carnations, lavender and mint, gladioli, fuchsia and nightscented stock romped in a confusion that was a glowing patchwork of colour, and the lazy drone of the bees and clacking of the cicadas filled the air with sound, as the perfume filled her senses.

'I suppose I should get the painters in,' Hudson said. 'But somehow I keep putting it off. The house and garden set in the native bush here has so much of her personality still, that I almost expect to see Sarah walking down the path to greet me.'

'Who lives here?' Serenity asked carefully.

'My married couple, Tessa and Lee, and their five children. They are away on holiday at the moment.

You'll like them, they're a beaut family, and she loves this old house.'

'I'm glad you didn't paint it,' Serenity commented as she wheeled Misty away. He must not know that she was so deeply moved that to stay there another second without claiming Sarah for her own would have been impossible. She was glad it was empty. She would come back on her own and sit on the sun-drenched verandah and soak up the impressions of the past, and feel the imprint of Sarah's personality seep into her being and sooth out the raw edges of grief and loss that were threatening to overwhelm her.

As Hudson caught up and rode beside her he demanded in concern, 'Are you up to this ride? You look so pale you're almost transparent. We can go tomorrow—there is no rush, as you'll be here for quite a while yet. I think you should turn back and have an hour or two in bed.'

'I look pale and wan and unattractive because I have just finished a stint on night-duty, and I think it's far from complimentary for you to keep flinging it at me,' she said with asperity, glad that her broad-brimmed hat shaded her eyes from his penetrating gaze.

'I think nothing of the sort, that you're unattractive I mean. As a matter of fact when you sat gazing at the house you reminded me of Sarah in the strangest way, the same long slender neck, the same beautifully moulded high cheek-bones and exquisite profile, but there the resemblance ended. You've got a waspish tongue and a perverse nature, not at all like my Sarah.'

Serenity chuckled, 'Glad you noticed, so don't try to bully me. I am perfectly well and I want to enjoy this ride. It's such a glorious day. Like the song, some days are diamonds, some days are stones.'

'Okay, Paleface, be it on your own head. Follow me.'

He flicked the reins and his big black horse broke into a canter and then a gallop.

Misty tossed her head impatiently until Serenity urged her on and as the horse lengthened stride she felt the joy of the rhythm and speed of the chase as the wind whipped her hair and face. Down the gravel road they galloped, past the stockyards and through the open gate then out across the green pasture. The thrill of the ride blotted out the past, and blurred the future, leaving her to concentrate on trying to catch the big man and his big horse and his retinue of dogs.

As he slowed to a canter she joined him, breathless and laughing. 'That was marvellous.'

'Good, although a bit unfair, Rajah runs the legs off your mustang. We'll have to give you something better.'

As they rode through a clear mountain stream and into a stand of magnificent *rimu* and *kahikatea* forest giants and elegant tree ferns the horses slowed to a walk, enjoying the shade and shadow of the cool green depths. Native birds were everywhere, pigeons and tuis, fantails and mocking-birds and their liquid song-notes hung on the air.

They emerged suddenly on the grassy bank of a wild and beautiful river, flowing deep blue-green and broad from the mountain gorge towards the sea, the surface so smooth that until she saw the white-flecked water and whirlpools as it forced its way against some rocks she had thought it calm.

'The Haupiri. It looks peaceful enough today, but you should see it in a flood. It would scare you then. We only get about two hours to clear the riverbed when it starts to rain heavily, then down it pours, bank to bank carrying everything before it, a raging torrent that nothing can survive. It's master here.'

'I thought you were,' Serenity commented.

'I would be foolish to think so. Most West Coast rivers are like this one, fierce, untamed and treacherous. My father, along with the Catchment Board, has spent literally thousands of dollars on this beauty trying to cajole it, control it, and discipline it, but he'd be the first to admit that he'll never win the battle.'

'You sound almost proud of that,' she said, puzzled by his tone.

'I suppose I am. You always admire a worthy adversary. This river is like a woman, wild and tempestuous, incredibly beautiful, entirely unpredictable, lulling you into a false sense of security for a few well-behaved years, then with full strength and vigour it goes on the rampage, carving out new territories for itself, destroying established pastureland, threatening access roads. When it does that the challenge is on, and every piece of modern technology, huge earth moving machines and years of experience are thrown into the war to bring it back on course. Sure, I love it, but I watch it.'

'If it's so difficult, why not sell out and buy a place safe from flooding?'

'What a mundane mind you have. Where would be the challenge in that? Besides, all the sweetest and best land is riverbed country.'

Serenity watched the river sliding irresistibly by on its way to the sea, glorious in its wantonness and beauty. 'And the wife you're thinking of taking for yourself, is she like the Haupiri, tempestuous, unpredictable, a challenge?'

'No, she's none of those.' His hazel eyes glinted angrily.

'A mundane choice, perhaps?' Serenity questioned with a barbed tongue. 'Or is she like Sarah Tarrant, quiet, submissive, loving you in spite of your overbearing ways?'

'How charmingly put. No, she's not like Sarah, but then *her* model is not available today. It's a throw-away society. If it doesn't work, scrap it.'

'What a rotten attitude you have to marriage,' Serenity shouted at him, completely outraged by his remark, and not knowing why. 'And this girl you've got on appro. . . . does she know that you don't love her? Does she know that you're playing 'Eeny meeny miney mo' with her life, maybe I'll take her, maybe I won't?'

'Yes, she does,' Hudson said calmly.

'Well, all I can say is that she must be a right pathetic lump, but then she would have to be, wouldn't she, even to *consider* marrying you?'

He sat watching her thoughtfully, and his mouth quirked as he looked at her furious face, then he threw back his head and roared with unrestrained laughter, startling the birds from a nearby tree.

Serenity just glared at him, not in the slightest amused.

At last he controlled himself. 'You're incredible, like a bucket of cold water in the face on a frosty morning. Breath-taking, but refreshing. Come on, Paleface, let's find the horses. Follow me.'

CHAPTER THREE

SERENITY clucked Misty into action and resentfully glared at Hudson's broad back, refusing to admire the relaxed, easy style of his handling of the impatient Rajah: in perfect command, yet making it look so easy. Of course he knew exactly the attractive picture he made on that marvellous black horse, probably rode it for the effect alone.

He turned in the saddle to make sure she was coming, then as if reading her thoughts, he grinned and winked wickedly before turning away.

Still simmering, she rode cautiously along the river's edge past the heavy rock protection works and out on to the sand and shingle. Why was she so angry? Admittedly, he was a handsome brute and the sun glinted on his burnished auburn hair in a spectacular way, and his tall, tanned, slim-hipped figure, completely at one with his horse, blended into this rugged mountain land incredibly well. So what! There was nothing in that to bring her to boiling point.

His attitude to marriage? It had *nothing* to do with her. If some dim-witted female was prepared to sit quivering on the shelf, waiting for him to summon her to his bridal-bed, it was still none of her business. It just let the whole female species down, that was all. But then Serenity herself wasn't an ardent feminist, so there was nothing there for her burning anger to feed on.

'We'll cross about half a mile up; the river divides into several streams and there is no danger. We'll just have to ride till the horses show themselves. They could be in the gorge on a day like this, or conversely down by the bridge three or four miles down river. Enjoying yourself?'

'Yes, thank you,' she answered primly. She was having trouble with Misty now that they were riding side by side. Misty kept edging closer and closer to Rajah until Serenity was riding knee to knee with Hudson.

'Don't fight her,' Hudson offered. 'These horses work a lot together and are friends. You'll battle her all day if you try to keep a respectable distance between them.'

'I suppose you picked them for us today for that reason.'

There was laughter in his voice as he answered, 'Of course. I didn't know how well you could ride. I want to be close enough to haul you back on the saddle if you look like cartwheeling into the drink. I don't like getting my feet wet.'

'A real hero,' Serenity observed nastily.

'Oh, I wouldn't say that. But we get droves of people out here. Most of them go gaga about the scenery, and all of them say they can ride like an Apache. We used to accept their words, but have learnt over the years, after a few nasty accidents, that people are prone to exaggerate their accomplishments.'

'Well, I didn't,' Serenity said indignantly.

'No, you didn't. I can see you're a fairly accomplished rider, but you're in unknown country, and until you're familiar with the terrain, it's better to be safe than sorry.'

It was a perfectly reasonable explanation. It showed sound common sense, and she was furiously angry with him all over again, for no reason. He had not been patronising, and she did feel much safer crossing the streams on the up side of Rajah. Although the crystal-clear water only came up to the stirrups the current was swift and strong, and in the wider parts had a mesmerising effect on her.

'Give her her head,' Hudson advised. 'She's a real river horse, and she'll pick her way over with the skill of a ballet dancer.'

'Sure.' Serenity wasn't frightened, but she was aware that there was danger and that she must balance her weight so as to be a help and not a hindrance to the surefooted horse as it negotiated the big boulders and loose shingle on the river floor.

There was colour everywhere, the vivid blue of the sky, the purple forest-clad surrounding hills, and gold everywhere; golden sunlight, golden gorse flowers, carpets of dandelions and buttercups. But green predominated, the thousand shades of green of the native bush, and the lush green of the grass on the islands where the sleek well-bred Hereford cows grazed with their enchanting calves, until disturbed by the horses. Then they crashed away and were soon lost in the *manuka* and low scrub.

'The horses can't go further up than this, we'll head downstream,' Hudson commented as the river neared the gorge with its steep rock-slid walls covered with bush and fern, and the streams blended and knit back into one deep strand of river.

'I didn't mean you to waste a whole day on me,' Serenity protested as they turned in the other direction. 'I feel quite guilty.'

His face creased into a smile. 'I'm not wasting my day. I had to come out and check on the feed situation here, and on the river. We've had a wonderful year climate-wise, abundant growth. The cattle love foraging out here and there's tons of feed. They'll be fine here for perhaps a month yet, which means I can make an extra paddock or two of hay, in case of a severe winter.'

'That relieves my mind.'

'I should have been gallant and protested a day in your company could never be considered wasted.'

'I prefer honesty,' Serenity told him crisply.

He chuckled. 'Well, I can be honest and say I am enjoying your company, and I can be honest and say the time has not been wasted, because I am also assessing your value as a future employee.'

'And are you impressed by my potential?' she demanded with a hint of sarcasm.

'Without a doubt, more and more each minute.'

'Huh!' Serenity had it on the tip of her tongue to say she was not going to stay under any circumstances, but she was still wavering, and decided to keep her options open.

'Taking on new staff out here is always a risk. Some people love the isolation, others loathe it. Then I have some young single chaps here and a flirtatious female could work havoc with my production schedule.'

'How do you know I'm not a flirtatious female?' she asked smartly.

'I trust my own judgment implicitly in these matters.' He was laughing again.

'And what does that mean?'

'Well, you're in love, engaged to, and planning to marry John. That's a big factor. You haven't tried to flirt with me, that's an even bigger factor. I find you a very cool number indeed, Miss Serenity James.'

'You're just not my type,' Serenity informed him casually.

'You don't have to flatter me just to get the job. I think my young male staff will be safe with you . . .'

'What an insult!' She was indignant. 'Safe indeed. How would you know? Just because you feel you are the quintessence of eligibility, and I find you lacking in appeal, you think I would not find anyone else attractive. There's no logic in that assumption.'

'I'll risk it,' he assured her cheerfully, not at all put out.

For the past hour Serenity had been trying to find a reason for her attitude towards him. If she could sort it out then maybe she could stay for a few weeks. When she thought of Sarah Tarrant's house she longed to stay; when she thought of riding this country most days, she longed to stay; and when she thought about Hudson Grey, she wanted to leave immediately.

How ridiculous! She shouldn't be frightened of him. Well, she wasn't exactly frightened, nervous perhaps? She had virtually no experience of men, and something told her that he was dangerous. But she couldn't see how he could be any threat to her. He thought she was engaged, getting married in six weeks even, and he said he wouldn't make a pass at her. He said that he didn't want complications in his life, that he was planning to marry soon himself. So why was she being such a ninny-hammer?

She had a God-given chance to stay here and get to meet all the people of the district. It was more than she had dreamed of originally, and she was dithering.

Because of Hudson Grey! *That's why she was angry.* Because she didn't trust him . . . and worse than that, she didn't trust herself. When he was arrogant and conceited it was a breeze to ignore him or take him down a peg or two, but when he had spoken about his mother and father and showed his open affection for them, then he was dangerous. And when he talked about Sarah Tarrant she saw beyond the smooth sophisticated surface to someone sensitive, and as vulnerable to hurt as she was.

She didn't want to see that side of him. She didn't want

to know him any better than she did at this moment. If she ever saw inside the pain and bitterness that was locked within him because of his girl's death, would she be able to walk away? Would she have the sense to leave well enough alone? Would she have the strength not to offer solicitude or comfort, the way her mother had helped, loved and healed people from hidden scars?

She glanced up at him as they rode and thought how little he knew about what appealed to some women. It wasn't his good looks, his essential masculinity, or his money, but the desire to comfort and cherish the hurt child in him that was her weakness.

'There you go.' He flung his hand out across the wilderness of riverbed. 'The horses.'

She gazed in that direction but all she saw was the cloud of a dust storm. Then her eyes widened as she saw the first horses plunge through the silver stream, the water spraying about them like jewels glinting in the sunlight. They were just as she had imagined them . . . quite magnificent.

'Will they come closer?' she asked breathlessly.

'They're full of curiosity—they'll come and give you the once over.'

And they did, dancing and prancing, cavorting and wheeling, their manes and tails streaming out from their glorious bodies, until they propped suddenly in a circle about the riders. Greys, whites, blacks, skewbalds and bays, their coats shining with good health, necks arched and flaring nostrils, eyes large and curious, they stood with flanks heaving for almost a full minute, then with the precision of a trained horse troupe wheeled and raced away and were lost from sight.

Serenity sat staring after them, half hoping that they would return. She was aware that Hudson was speaking to her, but in her ears still was the thunder of the horses' hooves on the shingle.

'I'm so sorry. That was fantastic.' She took a deep breath. 'What were you saying?'

'Looking at your face, I don't have to raise my price to keep you here. Which one did you fancy?'

'The chocolate-brown one with the creamy mane and tail,' Serenity said without hesitation. 'What a dream of a horse . . . and fast. Did you see him go, just like lightning?'

Hudson laughed, 'Somehow I thought you'd choose him, he's my favourite, too.'

'You're going too fast for me. I haven't said I'll stay. I don't think it's wise for me to stay here,' she protested nervously.

'Name your objections. I think it's a great idea.'

Serenity tipped her hat back from her face, 'Look, you don't know the first thing about me. All your judgments are superficial. You don't know if I'd fit in here.'

'Yes, I do.'

'You don't even know if I can cook.'

'I'll bet even money that you're a fantastic cook.'

'I can't cook scones and that's a fact,' she said aggressively.

'Have you any other personality defects which you would care to mention at this time?'

'No, I have not.' She glared at him in exasperation.

'Then it's a deal. You've got six weeks in hand, I need a bit of breathing space. Forget about the scones, I've got enough to keep me a year even if I ate them for breakfast, lunch and dinner. I'll get Cam to run the chocolate gelding in tomorrow night. What are you going to call him? Milo?'

'Why Milo?'

'Well, that's what he makes me think of, hot and sweet

and richly chocolate-brown with a large dab of whipped cream floating on the top.'

'Yes, I'd call him Milo,' she smiled, delighted with the choice. Then she frowned. 'That's another thing. I wouldn't be here long enough for him to be broken in.'

'You'll be riding him two weeks from now. I know what's the matter with you, I've starved you to death. Seeing as we're on this side of the river, we'll ride up to the Homestead and grab a bite. It must be at least two o'clock. Come on.'

She nudged Misty into a canter following Hudson along a beaten cattle trail among low scrub and frondlike spicy-scented *manuka* laden with tiny delicate flowers. Then the ground became more open and the trees bigger, large limbed *totara* and *rimu* trees, wineberry and *konini*, spreading broadleaf and *kowhai*.

Hudson waited, holding a gate open for her, 'Not far now. Five minutes and I'll have the kettle on.'

Serenity rode through, then waited as Rajah chested the gate back into position and Hudson slipped the bar through. 'My father nearly shot a cattle thief at this very gate years ago.'

Serenity looked at him doubtfully.

'The honest truth. Wait till Dad comes home, he'll tell you stories about this place before it became civilised that will make your hair curl. You'll hear the nostalgia in his voice as he talks about the mustering, long-horned cattle then, not a fence from one end of the valley to the other, and you had to be tough to hold your land and your cattle. Deer were everywhere. Even when I was a kid you just went out of an evening and shot one for the larder whenever you needed one. It's different now.'

'You sound a bit nostalgic yourself,' Serenity commented.

He laughed. 'I suppose I do. But I can remember

seeing a herd of about a hundred crossing the flats one evening and that's a sight never to be forgotten. Or standing in the morning mist in May down the Seven Hundred and hearing half a dozen stags in full roar within a few feet of you, that's something else again.'

As they splashed through another clear mountain stream, its banks lined with flax and native *toi toi*, she thought of her mother who had probably loved this country just as much as Hudson and his father did, yet had lived in exile for twenty years. It must have cost her dearly never to be able to come back and visit it.

As they topped the rise by the cattle yards, she saw spread out before her another wide green fertile valley even more beautiful than the one she'd seen this morning across the lake. They cantered through paddocks of sheep and cattle towards a brick homestead set attractively on a terrace overlooking the flats.

As they hitched the horses to the neat white fence, Serenity was surprised to find the back entrance was a simple pleasing hacienda style, the small patch of lawn enclosed by a long low verandah along its length on the house side and bounded by small cabins and the length of the double garage on the other two. Flowers and shrubs and climbing vines softened the almost austere lines.

Serenity turned to Hudson as he flung open the gate. 'The house looked so big riding towards it and . . .'

Hudson grinned, 'That's my father again. He loved the original pioneer home when he arrived here, the one he brought mother to as a young bride, so much so that when they decided to modernise he kept the same simple outline and blended in the extra rooms in a series of split level units. He has such a feeling for the past that he kept the best it had to offer. He drove the builder mad but

when I show you around you'll see he achieved exactly
what he set out to do.'

'I love it.' Then an appalling thought struck her. Was
Hudson's father the man in the photograph? Was Hudson her half-brother? Was it feasible? They were neighbours, only the river between them.

Hudson had reached the door and turned to find her
still standing halfway along the path. 'What's the matter? Come on in.'

She stood where she was. 'Hudson, describe your
father to me.'

He gave her a puzzled look, then seeing her face came
striding back. Laughing down at her he said, 'That's not
possible in the short time we have at our disposal. He's a
real character, unique, an original. The mould was
broken after he was made.'

'I don't mean his character or personality. Physically,
what does he look like?'

'Oh, physically, that's easy. He's well-built, keeps
himself in shape, he's not as tall as I am, more your
height. He's a good-looking fellow, much like myself, of
course, dark brown hair, going silver. I'll show you some
photos when we get inside.'

Her relief was tremendous and she gave him a spark-
ling-eyed smile. 'That's marvellous.'

'Hey! You didn't think it was Dad . . . that patient you
nursed?'

'No, it wasn't him, that's a fact.'

'I'll bet it wasn't. You'd never forget him if you'd
nursed him. I'll bet even money that he'd be the most
difficult patient you ever tried to strap into a bed. The
experience would be indelibly printed on your mind
forever.'

'I thought the way you talked about him you thought
he was perfect.'

'Far from it,' he gave a chuckle. 'I wish you could meet him. You'd enjoy him, most people do. He may not be big in height, but in every other way he's big; in his thinking, in his generosity, in his loyalty. He's a man with ideals and a vision of the future. Not one of those flabby idealists who only dream. He makes his come true which often brings him into conflict with more sedate minds, but he's well able to take care of himself.'

She followed him into the kitchen.

'Take a chair. I'll see if Naomi and Bill are about. They're friends of Dad's who are keeping the house warm for them.'

She heard him calling through the house and walked towards the large picture windows which gave a grand view of the farm. This house had certain similarities with the one over the river, yet there was a subtle difference, a maturity, a harmony of good taste and elegance. Still not satisfied that she had pinpointed the area of variance she looked about her, then smiled. It was the woman's touch that was here and not there, the imprint of his mother's personality. It gave the place a loving atmosphere.

'Serenity James, meet Naomi Fairmont. Bill is away up the river fishing. It's his passion.'

The small dark-haired lady welcomed Serenity. 'Hudson tells me you're going to housekeep for him for a while. I am pleased; baching is no fun. I'm sure you'll enjoy yourself, but feel free to ring me any time you need advice, support or just a natter. I'll put lunch on. Oh, Hudson, good boy, you've put the kettle on. And there's Bill coming by the woolshed, excellent timing.'

Serenity flicked a reproving glance at Hudson, but he ignored it, and went on talking to Naomi. She had *not* said she was staying and he was wrong to announce it as official.

After a good lunch of cold meat, crisp fresh lettuce and tomatoes, they relaxed over a second cup of coffee.

'How long have you known my father, Bill?' Hudson asked.

'You know that, Hudson, nearly forty years—well, more really. We trained together as pilots during the war. I've been coming here regularly since then. Why?'

'And you've known him for the same length of time, Naomi. Serenity here asked me to describe him, just before we came in. Now, how would you answer that question? A short answer, please.' He smiled at them encouragingly.

'Impossible, that's how your mother describes him,' Naomi said laughing.

Bill drew on his pipe, 'That's a hard question. He's an incredible chap, very versatile, but basically I would describe him as a man of principle.'

Hudson nodded, seemingly satisfied. 'And Mother?'

Naomi spoke first, 'Charming.'

Bill gave it some thought, 'A better word would be gracious, she is a gracious hostess. I've seen her through the years, entertaining politicians, businessmen, foreign diplomats, local dignitaries, farmers, contractors and shearers, hunters and farmhands, and her manner never alters. She offers each and every one the same standard of consideration, courtesy and tolerance. An excellent woman.'

'There you go, Serenity, I offer them as my credentials.'

'Many fine families produce a black sheep. I'll decide for myself what good qualities, if any, are in you.'

Hudson grinned, 'You're a hard lady to satisfy. Oh, I promised you a photograph of Dad. Are there any handy, Naomi?'

'On the chair in the lounge I put several copies of the

Press report on him receiving the OBE in the New Year's Honours. I thought they might like them when they get back.'

Hudson pushed back his chair and quickly walked through to the lounge, where he picked up a paper and returning gave it to Serenity. 'Is he the one you're looking for?'

'I told you he wasn't.' She took the paper, again feeling a tremendous sense of relief that neither Hudson nor his father was in any way connected with her mother.

'Do you mind if I read this?' she asked.

'No, carry on. I wanted to ask when you two are thinking of going to the Glaciers. Today?' Hudson turned to the Fairmonts.

Serenity skimmed through the article. The award was for services to farming stretching back thirty or forty years. It was an impressive list: on Canterbury University Board of Directors at thirty-five, first man nominated from the Coast to the Meat and Wool Section of the Dominion Council of Federated Farmers, pilot with RNZAF during the war, on the Regional Development Council, instrumental in bringing power and telephone to this remote area, work for Jaycees, Lions Club, starting the stock section of the Provincial A. & P. Show, starting the Veterinary Clinic, the inspiration and driving force behind the building of West Coast Producer Companies, chairman of others, and on and on . . .

She sighed. Hudson had every right to be proud of his father and she didn't even know who her father was. She was very quiet as they rode back across the river and Hudson seemed content to ride beside her in silence. She knew he was determined that she would stay, and that he wasn't used to being thwarted, but his opinion didn't worry her. Her own indecision hung like a heavy weight upon her.

When they stopped at the stables, Hudson dismounted. 'I'll fix the horses. You nip up to the house, have a shower and a rest. I'll call you when dinner is ready.'

'Thank you for a lovely day. I've enjoyed it very much. I'm not too tired, so if you tell me what you'd like for dinner, I'll cook it.'

'You'll cook my meals when you're paid for it; until then you're my guest.'

Serenity turned away without speaking and started up the road to the house. He was an impossible man, and if he ordered her round now, when she was his guest, working for him would hardly be a joy. If her car was here she would just get in and drive like fury away from the Bar 2 station, away from Hudson Grey, and away from any clinging mysteries of the past.

But where would she go? This valley had been her objective, and it was beautiful beyond description. As she reached the house, she stood looking down to where the lake shone blue and silver in the late afternoon sunlight, then keeping her gaze on the horizon she turned in a full circle. Blue, purple and shadowed, the bush-clad hills encircled the Station, giving it a protection from the world outside, secluded and peaceful, and above the fold upon fold of hills reared the snow-crested giants in awesome majesty.

She showered and changed into a simple sleeveless blue dress with a white collar, then lay on her bed for a short rest, but fell asleep immediately.

The slam of a car door brought her out of a deep sleep so abruptly that she was completely disorientated. She sat for a moment on the edge of the bed until her mind cleared, then walked to the window overlooking the patio. Hudson was talking to a tall, rangy man, wearing blue jeans and a Western-style stetson hat, and in his hand he held a coiled rope.

The horse-breaker. Hudson Grey was a fast mover. He was trying to put her under an obligation to stay, Serenity thought resentfully. Well, that was his misfortune. When he used steamroller tactics it made her less keen to stay.

Just then, the young man strode to the gate and as she turned to latch it glanced up directly at Serenity and lifted his hat with a smile. She gasped, her hand flying to her mouth to stop her making a sound, and she stepped back quickly. It was her photograph come to life, only this was in living colour, neatly trimmed bright gold hair, vivid blue eyes and strong sensitive features.

She waited till she heard the utility door slam and the sound of the engine die away before she went down the stairs.

'Just in time,' Hudson greeted her pleasantly. 'I was going to call you, but Cam held me up. The steak will be ready in two minutes. I'll mix you a drink. Take a seat.'

She obeyed him automatically, sitting on the edge of her chair, nervously fingering and smoothing her lace collar.

He placed a long cold drink in front of her and raised his own glass. 'Here's to our first meeting.'

She held up her glass in a return salute then took a drink as he moved back to the stove where the steak spat and sizzled. The fiery concoction steadied her a little. 'I thought I heard voices.'

'Young Cameron Blair. He's quick off the mark—he's got Milo down in the yards already. He'll start work on him in the morning.'

Serenity tried to quell the rising panic. She had to get away from here, she had been a fool to come. Her mother had never come back, and she had been wise.

'Steak dinner for two.' Hudson slid her plate in front of her.

'Does he live far from here?' Serenity helped herself to the side salad as if it was the most important thing in her life.

'Who? Oh, Cam . . . not far, ten miles or so. He's Robert Blair's son, the eldest. Now Robert could probably help you find your ex-patient. Their family has been here since the year dot. Might even be one of them as he had a couple of sisters and they are married up North. I'll run you up there tomorrow.'

Serenity choked and coughed. 'Sorry about that.'

Hudson half rose from his seat, then, seeing she was all right, said, 'Don't you dare infer that my steak is so tough it choked you.'

'No, it's fine, beautifully cooked.'

'Good, now where were we? Oh, the Blairs, they came out here in the horse and buggy days, about the same time as Sarah and Old Tom.'

'Did the Tarrants not have any children?'

'One daughter, but I can't remember her name. In fact I can't even remember seeing her. Still, when I was a kid Old Tom was running a feud with Dad so the families didn't have too much contact. I told you he fought with everyone. But he got over it, he had to later on, because he was so stroppy he couldn't get anyone to work for him, so he had to swallow his pride and get Dad to give a hand. That's how I came to know Sarah.'

'And even though you were friends she never talked about her daughter to you?' Serenity prompted him. If she was leaving tomorrow she wanted to learn everything she could from Hudson tonight.

'Only once and that was the night I brought her home from his funeral. She talked a blue streak, as if his death had released the safety catch on all the emotions that she had locked away for years. Not that she criticised her husband, she would never do that . . .'

He finished his steak, then smiled at Serenity. 'Now for dessert. You can have a choice, ice-cream and fruit, or fruit and ice-cream?'

'Ice-cream and fruit, please.'

'Good, a wise choice. My staple diet is ice-cream, with fruit in summer, and with apple crumble or steamed pudding in the winter. See how easy I am to cater for . . . aren't you glad that you said you'd be my housekeeper?'

'I haven't said I would be staying.'

He took her plate over to the sinkbench and went to the fridge before coming back with a large bowl of preserved apricots and a carton of ice-cream. 'It was a foregone conclusion.'

'What was?' Serenity sat up a little more erect in her chair.

'That you would stay here, of course,' he replied complacently.

'You're wrong. I have decided to leave in the morning.'

'And that's an irrevocable decision?' His eyes were lit with amusement. 'With Milo already in the yards?'

'If there were ten Milos in the yards I'd still be leaving.'

'How?'

'Somehow,' she said grimly. 'I'll walk if I have to.'

'Wedding dress and all?'

'I'll give you the wedding dress. Your girl will need *something* nice if she's going to marry you.'

'For a girl named Serenity you spark very easily. Tell you what, you sleep on it. If you still want to leave tomorrow, I'll take you into town.'

'Thank you,' she said smoothly.

'Now eat your ice-cream.'

She glared at him, 'I'm not a child. I don't need to be told to eay my ice-cream. I *do* know my own mind.'

'I know that you're not a child.' His green-brown eyes roved wickedly over her figure.

Serenity felt her colour rise and picked up her spoon and concentrated on her dessert.

'Tell me a little about yourself, Serenity. I've talked all day about the Station, my parents, my life, and all I've had from you is that your mother died eighteen months ago, and that you're going to marry John.'

'I told you also that I was a nurse and that I had a pony when I was young. Compared to you I've led a very dull life. I would much rather you told me more about your neighbours, about this district. I find it so interesting.'

'No, you don't,' Hudson said flatly. 'If you were interested you would accept my offer and stay. Let's forget the whole idea.'

Serenity bit her lip to stop her from pleading with him. It would be no use . . . she could tell that by his voice.

'Am I permitted to do the dishes?' she asked as she finished her coffee.

'Good idea. I've got some phone calls to make, then an avalanche of paperwork I've got to get through.' He got up from the table and strode towards his office without a backward glance.

He hadn't sounded rude or angry, just plain bored with her. She felt her spirits sag. Well, she deserved that. He had been really very kind and hospitable, he had offered her every inducement to stay, and she had refused.

She cleared the table, washed the dishes and put them away then wandered down the track towards Sarah Tarrant's house. At least she would fulfil her wish to sit on the verandah for a while. She wandered around the garden, loving the heady perfume from the gorgeous old moss roses and banks of lilacs, delighting to identify the small pansies, the golden mass of marigolds. A bank of dahlias, Sweet William and forget-me-nots added to the riot of colour.

The last rays of the setting sun tipped the mountains with pink and orange, and a gentle breeze ruffled her hair as she sat on the front step. What a fool she was not to accept the chance to stay, but seeing Cameron Blair had unnerved her completely. She had not come to this valley to cause trouble, only to satisfy her own curiosity. She had recognised Cameron so easily. What if his father found it just as easy to identify her with her mother? She was not unlike her, and what turmoil she would stir up if her guess was right. He was married with a family, and he wouldn't want the past confronting him in such a devastating manner. He wouldn't know that she had only come to look and didn't want to disturb his present life. She could do untold damage without meaning to. But, she longed to stay, and she had blown that chance too. Hudson Grey wasn't a man to string along. He wouldn't ask her again, and her depression deepened.

'Thought I'd find you here!'

She looked up to see the man who had been in her thoughts striding up the path towards her, and she knew her smile showed her pleasure.

He sat beside her, stretching his long legs comfortably on the steps. 'I've got a real problem now. The shearers have just rung. They were not due for another week, but they want to come midday tomorrow. I've let all my staff go for a couple of weeks off. The seasonal work was right up to date. I can recall the boys but Tessa and Lee are in Nelson caravaning—may have left by now. I've got no way of contacting them.'

'Why tell me?' Serenity asked, but her heart was

thumping, because she was sure he was going to ask her just once more.

'Well, the shearers usually bring their own cook, and she's not available. They asked did I have anyone to fill in. Naomi and Bill have already left for the Glaciers, not that I could have asked Naomi—she doesn't keep good health, and it's fairly hectic feeding that mob. Would you consider staying just four or five days? I'd like to take the opportunity of shearing a week early.'

'I mightn't be able to cope. I've never done catering on a big scale.'

His face lit in a smile. 'I'll give you as much help as I can. But you've got to be definite . . . I've got to ring them back immediately. Yes or no?'

'Yes,' Serenity flung all her doubts to one side. She could stay a few days and probably not meet Cameron or Robert Blair.

Hudson gave a whoop, and leapt to his feet, 'Great! You're a little trimmer.' He bent swiftly and planted an enthusiastic kiss on her upraised face and hurried down the path, vaulted the gate and disappeared from view.

Serenity sat there bemused, her hand going to her mouth, feeling again the warm firm pressure of his lips on hers. It had only been a way of saying thank you . . . certainly not to be classified as a pass, yet her heart was singing as she slowly followed the road home.

CHAPTER FOUR

AWAKENED by the thundering on her door long before dawn, Serenity groaned, rolled over and snuggled deep under the covers. She must have been crazy last night to insist that she would go over to the Homestead with Hudson and prepare the woolshed for the shearers.

But she had *insisted*, against his advice to stay in bed and drive over after lunch to prepare afternoon smoko and dinner. With every muscle screaming after her unaccustomed hours in the saddle yesterday, she staggered through to the shower, reviving a little under the force of water. She tried to recall her words of the night before as she towelled herself dry and dressed.

'Don't be ridiculous, a little ride won't have any effect on me. You have to have the woolshed set before daylight. Well, I volunteer to scrub that woolboard you're talking about while you get on with all the other jobs you've mentioned. Nurses are used to long hours, and scrubbing things. I insist.'

Huh! She walking stiffly down the stairs and said with forced brightness, 'Good morning, Hudson.'

'Oh, there you are. Cup of tea on the table. Where's your bag? I told you to throw a few things together in case we stay on the other side tonight.'

'I'll get it.' Gritting her teeth, she climbed the stairs, grateful that she had at least packed it last night, when she had been unable to sleep.

He was whistling cheerfully when she returned to the kitchen. 'Are you always this cheerful in the early hours?' she demanded in an almost accusing voice as she sipped the cup of tea he had poured for her.

'Always.' His mouth twitched. 'Having second thoughts? You can go back to bed for a couple of hours if you like.'

'And miss the best part of the day?' She wondered why the words didn't choke her. He looked so revoltingly efficient and healthy. Just how could she have ever thought him attractive? 'Anything I can do to help?'

'No, everything's under control. Finish your tea while I toss your bag in the truck. You said you couldn't bake scones so I've packed these two cartons with deep frozen scones, some pizzas and fruit loaves. You'll find them a godsend for smokos. We'll transfer them to the freezer over there.'

'I appreciate your supreme sacrifice,' Serenity said sarcastically.

He laughed. 'Oh, I fully expect you to replenish my hoard before you leave.'

'Always the optimist,' she flung after his retreating figure, and swallowed her tea hastily, almost scalding herself. She glanced at the clock and shuddered—four-thirty—he needed lynching. She made her way out to the Subaru truck, eased herself into the passenger seat, and closed her eyes. Fantastic.

When she opened her eyes she saw Hudson outlined in the doorway of a huge woolshed which was lit up like a battleship on a dark sea.

'You've had an extra twenty minutes sleep, are you ready to function now?'

By sheer will power she joined him, hugging her arms against the bite of the cold, glad of her thick jersey. 'Which board do you want scrubbed?'

'Sure you're up to it?'

'Of course I'm up to it!' she cried indignantly.

'I've thrown a couple of buckets of water on it to soften the dirt. Sorry it's such a mess, but we just haven't had time to get back since the crutching. I've got a couple of bales to press. There's a hot water cylinder there, buckets, brushes and detergent.'

She ran a bucket of hot water, tipped in the detergent and surveyed the filthy wet board with distasteful eyes and wrinkled nose.

'It's got to be spotlessly clean before they can start, so don't spare the water. It will have time to dry before midday as there's a nice easterly rising.'

'Nice easterly! That wind is colder than a stepmother's breath,' she observed sourly.

'You'll soon warm up with all that scrubbing,' he said callously.

Taking a deep breath, Serenity rolled up her sleeves and started. A quarter of an hour later she was so warm that she stripped off her jersey, and as her ring was hurting her finger she took it off and hung it on a huge nail by the louvre window at the end of the board. Another twenty minutes passed and her wet jeans were clinging and hampering her efforts. She went out to the truck and stripped them off, pulled on a brief pair of shorts and kicked off her sneakers. The dawn was breaking and she would have loved to stay and watch the shadowed valley come alive, but she wasn't even halfway up the board yet. It was a mile long.

As she crossed to refill her bucket there was an appreciative whistle from Hudson. '"Serenity James has a figure divine, and Serenity James is mine . . . all mine." If only John could see you now.'

Serenity laughed. 'I doubt he'd want me . . . he's a pretty fastidious guy.'

She set to work with enthusiasm, wondering how she could take such satisfaction from the clean smooth expanse behind her. She was aware that Hudson never stopped, his strong energetic figure moving from one task to another with tremendous vigour and efficiency.

'Howzat!' she demanded triumphantly as she flung the last bucket of boiling water down the vast length of the wooden boards.

Hudson strode over to examine her work. 'Fantastic. You've done a terrific job. It's as immaculate as an operating theatre. You're a credit to your profession, Serenity James.'

She beamed on him, warmed by his praise. 'You haven't done so badly yourself.' Her eyes roamed over the tidy floor and wooltable, the empty bins waiting to be filled, and the two newly-pressed bales sewn and stencilled in the far corner. 'Anything else you want me to do?'

'I've nearly finished here. It'll take me a few minutes to put on a new grinder paper, check the gate catches and fill the oil cans, then I'll be ready for breakfast. You nip over to the house and have a shower, and put some bacon and eggs in the pan. I'll be there by the time they're cooked.'

It took Serenity a little time to find her way around the kitchen, but she was just ready to serve up as he walked through from the bathroom.

'That smells great, and you look delicious too, but I prefer you in shorts.'

'Keep your mind on your food,' Serenity told him severely. She was glad she had been a nurse and was used to blatant, meaningless compliments from the men patients. She knew how to keep them in their place, but Hudson Grey was a different proposition. He wasn't sick; in fact, he was dangerously healthy.

'Yes, we'd better concentrate on food. Grab a biro, and we'll make a list while we eat. I told Gary to call at the Store and pick up the mail, milk and groceries. If we ring soon, it will give them time to pack the extras. It will mainly be bread and fresh vegetables. Mother keeps everything well stocked up here, and I can send the boys back across the river if we hit a crisis.'

Her list lengthened, and her eyes opened at the massive quantities being ordered. 'If they eat all this, they won't have time to shear,' she protested. 'How many are coming?'

'Four stands means four shearers, four fleecies, one presser, and two rousies. Then there's you and me, and the two boys, say fifteen or sixteen, and there's rarely a day passes at this time of the year without visitors. Still, they've eased off a bit with the parents away, praise the Lord.'

'And your mother copes with this every year.'

'Twice a year for shearing; then there's crutching, hay-making, and then the steady flow of stock and station agents, buyers, fencers and contractors.'

'All by herself?'

'Basically, yes, but don't panic—we'll make allowances for your being a beginner. Now, times are important. Meals and smokos ready on the dot. Wait till you see them go; they work under tremendous pressure, and burn up enormous energy. They need good, well-cooked food, and plenty of it, and to have it ready when they are. There's nothing more calculated to throw a spanner in the works of a harmonious shed than a bad cook.'

'If I had a hat, I'd take it off to your mother. If I saddle a horse and have it standing by for a quick getaway, I'll feel a bit more confident.' Yet she didn't feel scared. It was a new and exciting challenge, and she felt more vibrantly alive then she ever had before.

'There'll be horses saddled continuously until this is over, but I advise you to pick a fresh one if you intend to

outrun hungry, angry shearers, and I'll be moving myself, if you let me down.'

Serenity laughed as she pictured herself, fleeing down
the road on Misty, flecked with sweat, pursued by
fourteen or fifteen outraged, starving men. 'I'll grab a
gun.'

'You'll need it,' he said succinctly. 'Now we'll check
the freezer, take the meat out for dinner, then you clear
up here while I ring the Store. After that we'll bring the
first mob into the yards to empty out, before clearing the
cattle through. Any questions?'

'What do I do with visitors?'

'Ignore them. They won't expect to be entertained if
they come at a busy time. The majority will muck in and
give you a hand.'

As they caught the horses and loosed the dogs, Serenity said, 'Thanks for giving me a rough idea of the
quantities of food you're expecting. How come you
know such a lot about housekeeping?'

'It goes with the territory. Provisioning is a basic part
of Station life. There's no corner store to nip out to, or
fish and chips. You get accustomed to ordering in bulk;
I've grown up with it, it's a second nature. Dad's away a
lot on business, and sometimes he takes Mother, so I've
been through this enough to make it familiar.'

Serenity mounted a pleasant-natured skewbald, while
Hudson battled a large, spirited bay who bucked violently for about five minutes before settling into a steady
pace.

'Dicer's got to get it out of his system,' Hudson
remarked as they pulled up at the first gate. 'He'll be
okay now.'

'I'm glad I didn't draw him. It wouldn't have been
much of a contest. Oh, do I have to make up beds for
them?'

'No, they use the cottage and bring their own bed rolls. Let's zero in on these woollies.'

The next four days passed in a blur of men, meals, dishes and tiredness, and Serenity enjoyed every new sensation and experience. She was as familiar with the well-designed kitchen, by the last day, as if she had been born in it, and she blessed the luxury of the automatic dishwasher. Without it she would never have coped with the sea of dirty dishes. Each day as she plunged into the freezer and came out with a daily ration of scones and fruit loaf, she had loving thoughts of the previous house-keeper. It meant she only had to bake fruit cakes and biscuits, and make sandwiches, to fill the smoko baskets which came back from the shed as if they'd been tipped into an automatic disposal unit.

'Last day, Serenity. Do you think you'll hold together?' Hudson asked as he pushed the tray of chops into the oven, ready for breakfast.

'What a question! I'm thriving on it. They're great boys to cook for. They compliment me on everything I put in front of them, even if once or twice it has had the appearance of a burnt offering. They've got a great sense of humour. I love the way they chip each other. It's so funny, and there's no malice in it.'

'They've got a sense of humour, all right. I heard them invite you to become their permanent cook,' Hudson remarked dryly. 'Are you going to take them up on it? It's good money.'

'Only if you'll come with me,' Serenity informed him cheerfully. 'I'd never make it in the mornings if you didn't dig me out on time, and then help me cook breakfast. Mornings aren't my best period.'

'I've noticed. Still, you are improving. You're even smiling, and it's not six-thirty yet. A good effort; I'm grateful. And you've handled their barracking as if to the manner born. I'm full of admiration.'

Serenity laughed, 'Nursing is a pretty harsh training school for the sensitive in spirit. Still, I don't deserve all the credit. You really have babied me, easing me through, and sending Cam over ahead of them each day to help me carve and dish up.'

'He's a good chap, Cam. Look out, here they come. Stand to your mark, and don't fire till you see the whites of their eyes.'

When they streamed out again, Serenity sank into a chair and poured herself a cup of tea, surveying the chaos. Only one smoko to go, and then lunch, and that was the finish. Today the steady stream of sheep passing by the house would cease, woolly ones going up the hill, clean, shorn, white and sprightly ones moving back down. Excited barking dogs would quieten, and weary men and horses could rest from the demanding pace they had held.

'I must get my ring,' she admonished herself out loud. It was still hanging on the nail where she had left it the first morning. Each night before she fell asleep she remembered it, but during the day she never thought of retrieving it.

Serenity had only managed to get over to the shed a few times and had been so intrigued with the work that she had forgotten all about her ring. She always noticed the shearer's watches on nails above their heads, and once mentioned it to Hudson, where he worked at the wooltable classing the fleeces. He had confirmed that they were perfectly safe, even if left overnight. It had been her intention to get her ring that day, but she had stopped to watch the gun shearer on the first stand peeling off the fleece, with such precision and speed that she had needed a reminder from Hudson to send her flying back to the house to prepare lunch.

'Who are you?'

Serenity jumped nervously and turned towards the door where an extremely beautiful dark-haired girl stood impatiently.

'Sorry, I didn't hear a car.' Serenity stood up. 'I'm cooking for the shearer's.'

'Bring me a cup of black coffee through to the lounge. I have no intention of sitting in that mess.'

Serenity watched with raised eyebrows as the girl slowly sauntered through to the lounge, stopping to flick through some mail on the sideboard, before sitting with great elegance in a huge armchair. Serenity hesitated. Hudson had said to ignore visitors and she was sorely tempted. She shrugged her shoulders and went to plug in the kettle. Somehow she felt people rarely, if ever, ignored this most sophisticated and assured lady.

She began to clear the table.

'Where are the Fairmonts? I expected to find them here.'

In spite of her irritated feelings Serenity had to admire the visitor's exceptionally well-bred voice and careful enunciation. Obviously the product of an excellent young ladies' school.

'They went to the Glaciers, the day shearing started.'

'They showed phenomenal good sense. Is that coffee ready yet? I've had a long drive.'

Serenity continued wiping down the table, then made a mug of coffee and carried it through.

'I prefer my coffee in a bone china cup, which you will find in the left-hand cupboard. I also suggest you use a tray with sugar and biscuits on it. Thank you.'

Serenity's grey eyes glittered as she stood, mug in hand, wondering how her visitor would cope with a hot dark stream of coffee pouring down her incredibly stylish cream dress and obviously hand-made Italian shoes.

She stood too long and her sense of humour overtook her.

'Sorry, ma'am. Nobody taught me to do things fancy like,' she flattened her vowels atrociously and bobbed a half curtsey, and giggled all the way back to the kitchen, where she prepared the required tray. This time it was accepted in silence.

Serenity quickly packed the dishwasher, and popped some scones in the oven. They would need half an hour to thaw. She filled the large kettles and started to make the sandwiches. She liked to have the morning tea well forward before tackling the vegetables for lunch.

Her visitor came through and stood by the table. 'They look rather nice, I'll try one. I think you're using a bit too much butter. Don't be so heavy-handed, it's not economical.'

Serenity continued with her work.

'Is Mr Grey over at the woolshed?'

'I dunno. Yeah, I s'pose Hudson is at the yards.'

'Did Mr Grey give you permission to call him Hudson?'

'Naw! I guess not. Everybody calls him Hudson, he's not stuck-up like some.'

She felt rather than heard her visitor twitch with annoyance and kept on with the sandwich making.

'That will change in the near future,' an icy voice declared.

'Yeah, well . . .' but Serenity was talking to herself and all that was left of the elegant visitor was a waft of an expensive perfume on the wind.

Serenity leaned round the door and yelled raucously, 'See yah, then!'

She grinned as she saw the figure stiffen in anger and then proceed at a more determined pace towards the woolshed.

'Wotchit, Mr Grey, darling,' she muttered then giggled hysterically wondering what made her behave in such a ridiculous fashion. She hoped the woman would leave before lunch because she would have trouble keeping up her act for long. Still, she had more important things to think about. Only two more rounds to go and then the bell would sound to finish the series. She wasn't going to spoil her record by worrying about some haughty madam.

When she saw Cameron Blair come in the back gate she waved happily. In only a few days she had really come to like him, a pleasant quiet young man, but not shy.

'Oh, Cam, when you take this over, will you have a look on the nail by the first louvre just in the side door? I hooked my engagement ring on it and then forgot all about it.'

'Sure. You mean at the end of the board where Jim's shearing?'

She nodded as she loaded him up with the morning smoko, and then went to check on the corned beef. Carrots, cabbage, corned beef and potatoes, that should hold them.

Cam was back almost immediately. 'I must have got the wrong nail. You'd better come and look for yourself. I can't see it there.'

'I'll come now, everything is okay here.' She enjoyed getting out in the sunshine even if just for a few minutes. 'Did you know the lady who was visiting Hudson this morning?'

'Yes, that's Madeline Buchanan. She's a lawyer, a very astute one too, from what I hear.'

'Are she and Hudson . . . er . . . close friends?'

'Very close, I'm told. She's his regular partner at any official functions.'

'That's peculiar. He's got great taste in dogs,' Serenity replied with a grin.

'Oh, Serenity, that's a terrible thing to say.' But he chuckled in spite of his protest.

'That's the one he *may* marry?' Serenity asked, appalled as the awful thought struck her.

'Everyone is expecting them to marry,' Cam offered, a bit doubtfully.

And she had called her a *pathetic lump*. She certainly wasn't that . . . Hudson was. 'She's got a splendid speaking voice.'

She was educated in England. I'm told she's brilliant in court. She lives and practises in Christchurch, but she's got a super car and makes it over here relatively often.'

They reached the shed door as Serenity thought happily that the next time her ladyship returned she would be long gone. She looked up confidently at the nail. It was so big nothing could fall off it.

But it was bare. Shocked, she stared at it, then climbed the stairs to run her finger along it. The ring had gone!

She felt sick in the pit of her stomach. How could she have been so careless? It was such a valuable ring. Perhaps Hudson had taken charge of it. She felt much happier. It would be just like him, taking it to teach her a lesson. She hurried over to where he was sitting with the men enjoying their morning break.

She edged around beside him and as he looked up she dropped to her knees beside him. 'Hudson, did you move my ring from that nail?'

'What nail?'

Her heart sank. 'That one by the first stand. I thought you *must* have taken it,' she said desperately.

'No, I never saw it. When did you put it there?'

'The other morning when I was scrubbing the board. It hurt my hand so I took it off. I just never seemed to get the time to get back to it.'

'You're a complete idiot. That ring must have cost the earth, well over a thousand dollars. I thought how that guy must love you to give you such a smashing great rock.'

Serenity nodded miserably. 'I know, I know . . .'

His face was dark with anger. 'To leave a temptation like that sitting there for days. You were encouraging someone to steal. Was it fully insured?'

'I think so.'

He got to his feet, towering over her, 'You only think so. Explain yourself.'

Serenity stood up shakily. She was aware that everyone was looking at her. Hudson had not raised his voice, but the very quietness of his tone seemed to accent his disgust. 'The jewellers' shop said something about them insuring it. I suppose they did. I won't know for certain until I ring them.'

'You realise by your careless action that you're going to throw suspicion on every person who works here, and all those who have visited during this period . . .'

Serenity glanced at the group at her feet, who had resumed their conversation, but their expressions showed concern. 'Please don't tell them. I'm positive none of them would take it. They're really nice . . . I think of them as friends,' she pleaded anxiously.

'They *are* my friends,' he said harshly. 'You leave me no option. To claim insurance you *have* to notify the police. I could . . .' He didn't complete the sentence, but there was no doubt what he meant.

He raised his voice. 'Can I have your attention for a moment? Miss James has just informed me that she has lost a valuable engagement ring. She hung it on a nail on the board the day we started shearing and now finds it missing. Show us the nail, please.'

Serenity walked the length of the board and reached up to touch the nail feeling every eye riveted on her. Hudson had shown his anger by calling her Miss James, and they would all know what a fool she had been.

'Now come here and describe the ring. I want to know if any of you saw it hanging there and when.'

Serenity swallowed the huge lump in her throat and walked slowly back fighting her tears. It wasn't the loss of the ring. It was the fact that Hudson and these men might be hurt by her stupidity.

'It had a sapphire, a big one in the centre and a tiny group of twelve diamonds encircling it. It was sort of oval . . .' She stopped, unable to go on.

As she stood looking at the board she was amazed to hear voices saying. 'Hard luck, kid.' 'Gee, that's tough.' 'Hope you find it.' She looked up and saw, not condemnation, but genuine sympathy. But not in Hudson's eyes. He condemned her.

'Well, anyone see it?' he demanded sharply.

Heads shook, shoulders shrugged, some looked at the nail, some at Hudson, some at Serenity, and some at the floor . . . all negative. There was a long silence.

'I'm not accusing anyone. I certainly am not going to because I consider Miss James to have been criminally careless to have taken such a risk with her property. The responsibility is hers, not mine. Most of you have been coming here for years and are trusted friends. All I want to know is did anyone see it on the nail. I just want confirmation that it was there, if possible.'

Serenity felt her heart lurch sickeningly. He didn't even believe her.

There was another long silence then a young rousie, Ben, stood up. 'I didn't see the ring but I've been thinking back to the day I arrived. We'd finished at Frazer's, and coming down on the back of the truck I put on my thick jersey because it was cold. It was my best one, so I took it off as soon as I got here, and I hooked it on that nail. I didn't see the ring, honest, I was in a hurry to help pen up. It could have been there, I just didn't see it.'

'Thanks, Ben, that's helpful. What sort of a jersey?' Hudson asked quietly.

'A thick Arran jersey. My mother knitted it.'

'Did you notice anything when you took it down?'

'No. I've been trying to think back. It had been a big day. I was completely b . . . sorry, whacked out. I think I just flicked it down and flung it over my shoulder. I didn't have the strength to put it on. I'm not used to this caper.'

'So a ring could have got hooked on your jersey without your knowledge. It may be still there. I'd be grateful if you'd nip over to the cottage at lunch time and have a look. Right, we've spent enough time on this enquiry, and I have no intention of interrupting your work. If anyone knows anything about the ring, whether they removed it themselves, or know of someone else who did, or if they find it, I would appreciate it if they would replace it on the nail. I give you my word there will be no further action taken if that happens. Clear this stuff away, Cam, then go and give Serenity a hand to cope with lunch.'

'There's no need,' Serenity said fiercely. 'I am quite capable of handling my job. Thank you all for being so kind and helpful.' She turned sharply away so that they wouldn't see her tears.

Ben caught up with her as she reached the back gate. 'Jim's the head of the shearing gang, not Hudson Grey. He said they could manage without me for five minutes and for me to take a quick look. I'm real sorry, Serenity, Jim is too. I'll stay back and give you a hand to hunt for it when we finish shearing. We'll find it.'

Serenity nodded at him, 'Thanks, Ben. It's not your fault.'

'I know that, but I'm just wishing that I'd picked any other darned nail in the shed. I'll run in with it if I find it, otherwise I'll go straight back to the shed.'

Why hadn't Hudson said he was sorry the ring was lost? She hated him for making her look such a moron in front of the men, and not even offering a word of sympathy. And he hadn't even believed it was there, asking for confirmation like that. Did he think she was pulling some sort of con job, that she was hoping to get money out of him? She had never liked him and his arrogant ways. People like him *never* made silly mistakes.

She put on the vegetables and made a huge apple crumble. It was easier to work hard than to think about the ring. What would John think about her losing it? *He* wouldn't think she had done it deliberately.

'Sorry about your ring, Serenity,' Cam said as he came in. 'I'll give you a hand to search for it when the gang leaves. Hudson sent me over to put the beer in the fridge. The pace has dropped a bit and they'll have to work another hour after lunch. Don't worry about afternoon smoko, they'll finish off on beer and a few sandwiches.'

'I suppose that's my fault too, the pace slacking off,' she said sadly.

Cam shrugged his shoulders. 'Something's taken the edge off them, but they won't blame you. Is there anything I can do to help you?'

'No, I'm right up with the play. I'm fine,' she answered with a forced smile.

Cam looked at her strained face and huge shocked grey eyes, 'Sure you're doing fine. I'll be back to give you a hand at five to twelve. Try not to worry.'

'Is Ben back in the shed?'

'Yes. He couldn't find it, but that doesn't mean it's not there. He only had time for a quick look. It could have dropped off his jersey anywhere between here and the woolshed. It'll turn up.' He gave her an encouraging smile and left.

Serenity turned back to the sink. Thousands of sheep had trotted backwards and forwards over that ground. It would be a miracle if it was still there.

She served lunch quickly and efficiently and spoke very little. The men were quiet also. Perhaps they were always like this at the end of a run, but she believed her problem had shadowed their normal good spirits.

As they filed out, Jim, the head of the gang, came over to her. 'Bad luck this ring business, Serenity. The boys and I really appreciate the way you've laid it on this week, you've really looked after us. We know that you just filled in, and it's a tough job, so accept our thanks.'

'I'm glad you survived my cooking in good shape,' she said with a pleased smile.

'We've done exceptionally well. Listen, I've got a mate who fossicks for gold. He's got one of those scanners that picks up metal in the ground and bounces the sound back. He has had exceptional success with it, and he helped a farmer I know. This guy and his wife were drafting sheep in the yards and she threw out her hand to block the sheep and her wedding ring, which was a bit large, flew off. The yard was all churned up and muddy, yet weeks later when they called Terry in, he only took five minutes to find it. It was buried about four inches in the mud but he spotted it no trouble.'

Hudson had joined them and was listening. 'Now, that's a brilliant idea, Jim. Who has it? Would he come out here with that gadget? I'm quite prepared to pay him for his time.'

'He wouldn't take money. He'd come like a shot, he loves to show what it can do. Terry Goulder, you'd know him Hudson.'

'Of course I do. He's been out here often. We'll have a bit of a look this afternoon, and if we don't find it, we'll call him in.'

Jim walked out and Hudson turned to Serenity. 'I talked to Jim on the way over. He can vouch for all his men except one new chap, so we may be lucky.'

'It wasn't Ben,' she exclaimed, then added harshly, 'You mean you actually believe the ring was on the nail?'

'I'll take your word on anything, Serenity.' He gave her a curious glance and walked out.

Suddenly she was swamped with guilt. She hadn't been completely honest with him. She had let him think her wedding had only been unavoidably postponed, that all was well between her and John. Well, it was none of his business really, but if he learned about that he would naturally start to doubt her word in other areas. Still, there was no way he could find out if she didn't tell him herself, and she wouldn't do that.

She started on her work strangely warmed by his words. He believed her. Why should his good opinion matter so much? Yet, it did. It was terribly important, more important than the finding of the ring. Appalled at where her thoughts were leading her, she immediately concentrated on her work.

She checked on the beer, made the sandwiches, and filled a carton with clean glasses. She wanted to leave the house in the same spotless condition she had found it.

She stacked the dishwasher, stripped the beds and gathered up all the dirty linen and loaded the washing-machine. She wanted to rush straight out and look for her ring, but kept doggedly on until the house was vacuumed and dusted, the kitchen, porch and wash-house mopped out and fresh flowers placed in the vases.

She walked through the house with a critical eye to satisfy herself that all was well, admiring as she went the way the magnificent native timber had been used so extensively throughout the building, especially the massive beams. Hudson had told her it had been taken from trees grown on the property. It was a beautiful home, pleasing in every aspect, from the architecture to the lawns, gardens and trees surrounding it.

Satisfied at last she walked out into the bright sunshine. As she searched the road and grass verges her mind was in a turmoil. What if the ring wasn't found today? Could she stay and look for it? Would Hudson allow her to stay? Yet how could she go away without searching every inch of the woolshed?

As she neared the woolshed Hudson appeared at the doorway. 'Come and have a farewell drink with the boys, Serenity.'

She wanted to refuse, she wanted to keep on looking, the very next step might reveal her ring, but it would look terrible if she refused.

'Love to, it's so hot out here.' She came into the shed, smiling even though it cost her considerable effort.

Everyone was talking about rings, lost ones, found ones; incredible stories but she knew they were true. One had been lost a year, another eight years, another nineteen years, but they had all been found eventually. She couldn't wait that long, though. It was a relief when they left, but Cam stayed back, and young Ben, the two boys Gary and Tim who were permanent staff, and herself and Hudson.

'Let's try an experiment,' Hudson suggested. 'Get me your jersey, Ben.'

Ben rushed out and came back with a thick Arran jersey knitted in natural wool.

Hudson took it, and slipping off a signet ring he always wore, he hung it on the nail, then hooked the jersey on top of it. 'Now Ben, take it down as you did that night.'

Ben walked over and flicked the jersey down and headed for the door. The ring flew halfway across the wool floor and bounced into a pile of skirtings.

No one said a word as Hudson walked to retrieve it, not without a bit of difficulty.

Silently they stared at each other. It could be in the wool, pressed and baled and ready to go for auction. *Thirty* bales of it, each weighing about four hundred pounds. An impossible task to find it.

'We'll try again,' Hudson said calmly. 'The best of three.' The experiment was repeated, and the second time the ring fell flat then rolled under the wool board itself which was about three feet high where all the oddments and bellies were thrown to keep them from spoiling the good fleece wool. Another mammoth job if it was to be searched, hours of work. The third time the ring repeated the centre bounce and landed against the wool press.

Serenity sighed with despair. 'There's no use looking for it. It's hopelessly lost.'

'Never say never, Serenity,' Hudson said cheerfully, almost as if the magnitude of the problem excited him. 'Let's consider it from all angles. What do you think happened to it, Cam?'

'After that exhibition, I'd say there's a fair chance it's buried deep in those bales, or second guess would be it hung on to the jersey, and got carried to the cottage, or part way there.'

'Ben, how about you?' Hudson asked.

'About the same as Cam's, but one of the gang could have pocketed it. If it was that classy, and sat there four days, it's a mighty big temptation. I'm not saying that happened but it's possible.'

'That's right, I want all the possibilities. Tim you're next, then you, Gary.'

'I'll pick under the wool board, because I'm naturally lazy and that will take less effort to sieve than the other lot,' Tim offered with a rueful grin.

Everyone laughed and Gary said, 'All that the others said, but I have an itching to search around the edges of the shed. Remember, it happened the first night, and there wasn't so much wool about like there is now. Secondly, your ring is large and heavy, Hudson, a man's ring. Serenity's ring, being lighter and a different shape, could have bounced or rolled further than yours.'

'Good thinking,' Hudson commented. 'And you, Serenity?'

'Forget it. I'll ring the insurance company,' she said glumly. There were just too many places it could have lodged.

'You do that. I'll come over to the house with you and ring the local police. I know them well. Tim, you go with Ben and give that cottage a real going over. Shake out the mattresses, blankets, mats, sweep the floor, do it thoroughly and we won't have to cover that ground again. Gary, and you Cam, if you're staying, check all the obvious places in here. I'll contact Terry and see how fast he can get out here. There's no use us spending hours if he can find it in minutes.'

Serenity packed up the glasses into the carton and tidied up the sandwich boxes to take home.

'I'll carry those, Serenity. Get a move on.' Hudson strode away making her half-run to keep up. 'It's Saturday—I hope your jeweller friend is open for Saturday shopping. You ring him right now,' he instructed, and 'book it to the Station. I want this cleared up pronto.'

Serenity had to find the number from the directory service, then placed the call.

'Did you make it person to person to the Manager?' Hudson demanded when she returned to the kitchen.

She shook her head.

'Then go and do so. You'll save time and money going straight to the top, and they'll get him at home if he's not at the store.'

She changed the call and it came straight through. She stated the position, gave the date the ring was purchased, and hung on.

'Are you there, Miss James? Look, I'm sorry, we've been through the insurance cards and can find no trace of your name or John Bellamy's name. Things have been a bit chaotic here and the filing system is not as up to date as it should be. If you bought the ring here and asked us to insure it, then I think you can consider yourself covered. All I'm saying is that I can't find proof and this call is costing you a lot of money. I'll ring back and confirm it when we find the record of purchase. Give me your number.'

Serenity gave the number. What else could go wrong? 'And you're positive it will be covered?'

'As positive as I can be without sighting the card. I'm new here, and the manager who has just left, let the place get into a shocking state.'

'You mean he was fired?'

'Yes. He was incompetent.'

'So, he could have forgotten to arrange the insurance?'

'I haven't said that. Just wait until I have time to check it out. I am aware how anxious you must be and will make every endeavour to sort it out today and get back to you as soon as possible.'

Serenity hung up and went out to speak to Hudson. Carefully avoiding his eyes, she gave him the facts in a flat monotone.

'I'll ring the Police,' he said quietly and went through the door closing it softly behind him.

She had expected an explosion, yet he had just walked away. When he came back she asked wearily, 'What happens now?'

'Well, it's obvious you have to stay here now. You've given this phone number to the jeweller, I've given it to the Police, Terry is coming out tomorrow afternoon, and is very confident. You're on my payroll now, and you'll stay on it until this mess is cleared up. Don't you want to stay?'

'Whatever you say,' Serenity felt completely defeated by the further complications; there seemed no end to them.

'You're tired out, so don't try to think now. Things will appear better in the morning. Pack your bags, and we'll go home. Clear up here and I'll put the last of the sheep away. Don't worry—it'll work out.'

The unexpected softness of his tone made her eyes brim with tears. 'I'm really very sorry this happened, Hudson.'

'That's okay, Paleface. I hired you for five days. You've panned out much better than I expected, you've kept up a cracking pace. I'd like to hire you for the next two weeks, no, until the end of the month. You'll get reasonable time off to come over here and hunt for your ring, but I'd like to count on you as a housekeeper for that period. There's haymaking ahead, the cattle muster, and I have to have someone I can rely on, someone who isn't threatening to leave every five minutes. How about it?'

She couldn't leave while there was a chance of finding the ring. It seemed the decision had been taken out of her hands and she felt relieved. 'I'll stay the month, then.'

He smiled down at her. 'It's a deal. Now, listen to me. When that manager calls back, I'm positive you'll find that you're fully covered and will be able to replace your ring before John returns. Only a reputable dealer would deal in rings of that quality, you can be assured of that. And I am also positive that we will find it. So stop worrying. Be ready in about half an hour.'

She watched him stride away full of confidence and was furious to find herself comparing his actions with the way John had behaved when she had had to face a difficult crisis.

John had slunk away shamefaced and left her to handle it on her own. Hudson had taken control immediately, not dodging the unpleasantness, and he had made the announcement without offending anyone, then continued on with responsible determination to cover all possibilities and details.

Even if she didn't like domineering men, she had to admit that he had carried most of the load for her, and at the same time had managed to inject a feeling of anticipation that it would all work out well.

She washed the glasses, and flew out to bring the clothes in, beautifully dry and sweet smelling in the easterly breeze. She tried to quell the surge of joy that filled her, but she couldn't help singing as she ironed the clothes and put them away.

Hudson *wanted* her to stay.

CHAPTER FIVE

'You can relax, now, Serenity,' Hudson said as he braked the Subaru by the back gate. 'No more cooking today. The boys will be across later, but they'll only stop long enough to shower and change. It's Saturday night, and they have big plans.'

Serenity got out and jerked her bag from the back. 'What about you? Won't you need a meal?'

'No. I've got to go out tonight, too. But I must shift some stock first.'

She watched him drive away, then walked inside feeling vaguely disappointed. She had been constantly in his company since she had arrived, and the house seemed empty without his overpowering presence. How ridiculous, she had only known him for five days.

She bathed and washed her hair, then, putting on a bikini because it was still very hot, she wandered to the far end of the lawn and stretched out on a seat. It was time she got a suntan—she was sick of being called Paleface.

Serenity brushed her long fair hair free of tangles, and lay down again to let the sun do its work. She felt restless and unable to relax. Her mind was overactive, flicking from subject to subject. She tried to focus on John. Where was he? What was he doing? Was he happy? She couldn't even remember the travel schedule they had spent many happy hours working out. She closed her eyes tightly, trying to picture his face, but all she saw was Hudson with his auburn hair and wicked hazel eyes smiling mockingly at her.

Resolutely, she thought about her car. She had been informed that the insurance company had written off the wreck, so she would buy a new one. If she had her own vehicle, she could have driven back to the Homestead and spent the evening looking for her ring. Still, the thought held no appeal. How was she going to fill the empty hours? Normally she loved having time to herself.

As the sun sank lower in the sky, she was shaded by a large tree, and that caused her to shiver, so she headed up to the house and made a cup of coffee for herself. Standing on the patio, she could see Hudson moving cattle down by the lake. He could have taken her with him, she thought resentfully.

Shocked by the trends of her thoughts, she admonished herself, 'Lady, the day your happiness depends on being in the vicinity of Hudson Grey . . . you've got big trouble on your plate.'

She would spend the evening with Sarah Tarrant. She would dress up and pretend she was going to visit her grandmother—it was a harmless enough fantasy, and next week Tessa and Lee and the children would be back.

Delighted, she went to her room, and pulled out her large case. What would she wear? Something very feminine. Yes, her grandmother had been a fine lady, so she would expect Serenity to dress correctly. Cheerfully she rejected all plunging necklines and trouser suits, and chose a chiffon dress, dreamy in pale green with dark green leaf patterns. And her hair, she would brush and brush it and twist it in a smooth knot at the nape of her neck, and she would wear stockings, cobweb fine, and shoes with an elegant heel.

Sarah Tarrant would greet her from the verandah, 'Come along in, Serenity James, and take tea with me. My, you've grown into a lovely young lady.'

It took her an hour to complete her careful toilet, and she twisted in front of the mirror, her eyes shining with pleasure. Her mother had always loved this dress, with its close-fitting bodice and flaring skirt, the dash of white lace at the throat and cuffs, and the twenty tiny looped buttons neatly fastened from the waist. Her coiffure was perfect, not a hair out of place, and her make-up was just right; eyebrows and lashes emphasised with mascara, the lightest touch of blusher on the high cheek bones, and lipstick. Now a dab of perfume, and she was off. She wandered through the shortcut she had discovered the first night, through the beech trees, and up the garden path.

She sat erect on the front steps, her hands folded on her lap, and her feet neatly placed—as a circumspect young lady would sit—and entered her dream world.

She heard a vehicle drive up some time later, and opened her eyes in time to see Hudson step out of a sleek, powerful car. He was looking fairly sleek and powerful himself, she mused, as she took in his immaculate dinner suit, the white shirt front complementing his tanned face.

'I knew I'd find you here,' he said cheerfully, easing his long frame down on the step, and adjusting the knife-edge crease on his trousers carefully.

'I always hide in the same place. I make it too easy for you,' she said with a smile.

'Oh, I wouldn't say that, Serenity James.' His hazel eyes laughed at her. 'May I say you're looking exceptionally lovely tonight?'

'You may,' Serenity returned his gaze steadily. 'You're cutting quite a dash yourself. No wonder the simple-minded village girls fling themselves at your feet.'

He grinned wickedly, 'You're not including yourself in that category?'

'No, I'm not,' she answered, as cool as the evening breeze outwardly, though her heart was thumping.

His hand stretched out to touch the froth of lace at her throat. 'You look so demure. Wouldn't you like to fling yourself at my feet? I think I'd enjoy the experience.'

He was too close for comfort. With a swift movement she was on her feet in a swirl of skirts. 'If I ever feel the urge, I'll restrain myself.' She walked over to the rambling old moss rose, and breathed deeply, loving the heavy perfume.

He followed and picked a bud from a yellow rose bush, handing it to her with a well-executed bow. 'This one is called Peace.'

'Thank you.' She accepted the rose. 'Do you need me for something?'

'What would your answer be, if I said I really needed you, Serenity James?'

'I'd tell you not to be silly, that you have everything you need already,' she said firmly.

'Yet you have the capacity to make me feel young again. To believe in all sorts of stupid things like purity, chastity, faithfulness . . .'

'What's so stupid about purity, or chastity?' Serenity demanded sharply.

'It's extinct . . . like the dodo. Like believing in fairies at the bottom of the garden; when you grow up, you know there aren't any. It's not a popular choice any longer . . . too old-fashioned.'

'Just because something is not popular is no proof that it no longer exists.'

'Well, I haven't met it for years . . .'

'You've met it tonight, so back down.' Serenity's eyes darkened dangerously.

'I could almost believe you. You're chock-full of surprises,' he laughed lightheartedly.

'You'll be in for some more surprises if you dawdle round here and leave your partner cooling her heels. She'll be wanting her pound of flesh.'

'So you know she's a lawyer. Did you see her this morning?'

'I saw her, but she didn't really see me.'

'And were you impressed? Not exactly the pathetic lump you envisioned.'

'Certainly not that,' Serenity agreed blandly.

'Well, what did you think of her?'

'I think that she should fulfil all your expectations,' Serenity declared solemnly.

'That sounds ominous. Which expectations are you referring to?'

'You're not offering love. You don't want it in your marriage. With her as your wife, I don't think you need to worry. Apart from that, it should be a fine arrangement. She is highly intelligent, well educated, of excellent social standing and, at a guess, wealthy.'

'And you didn't like her?' Hudson had a speculative gleam in his eye.

'I liked her as much as she liked me,' Serenity said firmly.

'But you think love is important?'

'Yes, I do. But then I'm not like you. Money, position, background are not important to me. When you offered me your credentials that first day, you gave me your parents' track record. I didn't even know my father, my mother was a doctor's receptionist, yet I feel no less a person than your Madeline Buchanan. It would be nice to have had the privileges that you have had and she has had, but I don't feel in the least deprived because

I haven't got them. It's what I make of my own life that counts.'

'Very commendable, but you didn't answer my question. Do you think love is important in a marriage?'

Serenity met his gaze steadily. She'd forgotten his habit of not letting go when he wanted information.

'Essential. But again, you and I have nothing in common. You think marriage is part of the throw-away society. I believe in the "till death us do part" contract. I want my marriage to last. I will work at it. I will bring everything I have to offer to make that happen, and I will choose a man who feels the same way. I have a good mind, and a good body . . .'

'I'll vouch for the body.' His mouth twitched.

'Don't be flippant,' she flared at him. 'You asked for my opinion, you're getting it. Marriage is more than loving, it's a commitment—of the mind, of the emotions, and especially of the will. You have committed yourself to this station. You don't cut and run when things go wrong; you stay and hold in there till you make it come right again. A professional soldier or athlete commits himself to a certain way of life, and when things are rough, he'll probably hate it, but he'll stay with it because it is his choice. It's the commitment that counts, but you can't carry it through without love.'

'And John feels the same way you do?' He looked at her curiously.

'Of course,' she snapped. Then honesty forced her to add, 'I'm sure he does. I've never spelled it out for him, but he never asked me, and you did.'

'I hope he's man enough for the road,' Hudson commented. His hazel eyes bored into her as if reading her thoughts.

Serenity bit her lip and looked away. John wasn't, but she wasn't going to marry John, only Hudson didn't know that. She didn't even know where those words had come from, but she knew for certain she could never marry John now. She did not love him enough.

'You know, Serenity, you sounded just like Sarah Tarrant. She used to lecture me just like that. I wish you'd met her.'

'So do I,' Serenity said passionately. 'You don't know how much.' Then, more quietly, she asked, 'I don't want to keep you. What did you want?'

'You're not keeping me. I'd like to stay and talk to you, but unfortunately I have a previous engagement, and duty calls . . .'

'If I ever had a date with you, and you called it unfortunate, or duty, I wouldn't be pleased.'

He grinned. 'If you ever have a date with me, I'd never describe it as duty, and certainly never regard it as unfortunate.'

'I told you I prefer sincerity to flattery,' she said angrily, stepping away from him.

'And you think I'm not sincere?'

Again there was that curious look in his eyes, and her heart started to pound. Something was happening here that she didn't understand, like the time he told her about his girl dying. She felt excited, and vibrantly alive, yet intensely vulnerable, as if she were swimming out of her depth. The heavenly fragrance of the garden and the gathering dusk combined to make her more aware of him than she had ever been of any other man. She wanted to run, yet knew she wouldn't.

'Oh, Cam is up at the house. He thought he'd visit with you in case you were still upset about your ring, and I thought you might be a bit nervous being left on your own.'

'You asked him to look after me?' Serenity demanded furiously. 'I don't need a baby-sitter. I *told* you, I like solitude. You're late. Why don't you go?'

'Because I'm enjoying myself. Sarah always walked to the gate with me. Are you going to walk me to the gate, Serenity?'

'Yes, I'll do that. Come on.' Anything to get rid of him, now. There was danger all around here; she sensed it. She didn't need to look at him to know that he was smiling. She led him by the hand, trying to urge him to hurry. If she could only get him into the car, she would be safe. Could he feel her trembling?

At the car he stopped, but did not release her hand. 'Oh, I meant to mention, Madeline will be staying here tonight, or what's left of it by the time we get home.'

She took a deep breath. 'That should be interesting.'

'Why do you say that?'

'Well, this morning she asked me if I had your permission to call you Hudson. Do you think I should call you Mr Grey while she is visiting?'

'Certainly not. I love you calling me Hudson.'

Serenity tried to release her hand, but he held it firmly, so she just stood looking up at him.

'Madeline is not used to West Coast ways. We don't stand on ceremony. She'll change.'

'No, she won't do that, Hudson. You'll be the one who changes.' It came out thickly and charged with emotion, and she cursed herself for giving so much away.

'So you like me as I am, do you, Paleface? What a delightful surprise.' He chuckled and pulled her closer.

She knew he was going to kiss her, and far from wanting to stop him, she wanted him to more than she had ever wanted anything before. With shining eyes and her mouth softening into a smile, she put her free arm about his neck and lifted her enchanting face to his, and gave herself to an experience that she knew would shatter her world into a million pieces. She knew in the moment before his firm lips came down on hers that she had fallen in love with Hudson Grey.

She had been playing with fire from the moment he had joined her in the garden, and now the fire was out of control, searing her, scorching her with its intensity, carrying her to heights that she had not believed existed. And she met fire with fire, feeling boneless and floating free, her hand in his auburn hair holding him to her, holding the moment so that time itself would cease.

At last he lifted his head and stared down into her eyes. 'I don't often make mistakes. I should not have asked you to stay.'

She felt his arms free her and she stepped back, away from him. 'I'll leave tomorrow,' she offered quietly.

'No. A deal is a deal, and anyway I think it's too late. I must go. Goodnight, Serenity James.'

'Goodnight, Hudson.' She watched him get into the car and reverse out to the track, then watched the lights sweep across the paddock as he took the road for town.

She turned her steps towards the house where Cam waited. So Hudson was sorry he had kissed her. Well, she wasn't sorry. She was glad, she was so glad. She felt shaken to the depths of her being, but now she had a yardstick, a measure to gauge her feelings. Unless any other man could make her feel the way Hudson had, she could not even consider marriage as a remote possibility, and she did not believe that such a man existed. Only Hudson.

Suddenly the moon rose over the snow-clad mountains, huge, round and golden, flooding the darkened valley with light, and she danced the last few yards to the house. Would Cam notice anything different about her? She felt an entirely different person, changed, more vital, impulsive, intoxicated with happiness. Would it show on the outside?

'Good evening, Cam. It was nice of you to visit me, but as I told Hudson, I'm not scared of being on my own. Don't feel you have to stay.'

'I won't. I had to come over and give Milo a few turns. He's coming on fine. He respects the rope now, and it's important to keep to a routine or I'll have to start all over again.'

She looked up at his tall, lanky frame. 'Is that your full-time work? Breaking in horses?'

'Hardly. It's my hobby. I love horses, and have always been good with them. I'm on vacation just now from College, so I've been working with Hudson on these horses, and enjoying it.'

'Agricultural College, I suppose?' she said as she went to plug in the kettle. 'Tea or coffee?'

'Tea will be fine.'

'Have you had dinner, Cam? Can I make you something?' She suddenly realised she was starving . . . so it couldn't be love. People in love didn't want to eat. Funny, it felt like love.

'I had a sandwich with the boys when they came in, but if you're cooking, I'm eating.'

Serenity laughed. 'How about an omelette?' She felt like singing, as if an orchestra was playing, swamping her with music.

'I'd enjoy that. Anything I can do to help? You look different tonight, Serenity. That dress is fabulous—surely you're not going to cook while you're wearing it?'

She had forgotten her dress, she had forgotten everything except Hudson, and his kiss. 'I'm not a messy cook. How do I look different?'

'Starry-eyed. Like someone in love,' Cam said, smiling. 'Hudson said you're getting married in a few weeks.

I know the feeling, but I've got to wait until I get my degree. By the way, I'm at Saint John's, in Auckland. I'm a theological student.'

Serenity turned in astonishment. 'You're going to be a vicar?'

His eyes were vividly blue. 'Don't you approve?'

'Yes, but it's such a surprise.' She continued to beat the eggs, and quickly poured them into the pan.

'It was a surprise to the family, too. They're getting used to it now, but Dad was fairly provoked by my decision. Eldest son, and all that, supposed to go on the farm. Still, I explained the old English style was to give one son to the Church, one to the Army, and the idiot son stayed on the farm.'

Serenity asked with a smile, 'Have you an idiot brother to fit the part?'

'Two, actually. No, they're very competent, but younger, so Dad will still have the running of the place for a few more years. He thought he was going to off-load it on to me.'

'Do you get on well with your father?' Strange how easy she felt with Cam, as if she'd known him all her life, yet she had been petrified the first time she had seen him.

'Oh, there's the ordinary friction that occurs in most families, but on the whole we get on well. I'm probably closer to my mother than I am to him, especially since this church business. She came from a church family, so she understands, while Dad thinks I'm just a good farmer going to waste.'

Serenity served the cheese omelette and listened to Cam talk of his family and his girl, only half listening, really, her mind busy with her own thoughts. She had come here, in the first instance, to trace her mother's family, and secondly to find the man whose photo her mother had kept, but falling in love with Hudson had eclipsed everything else. Suddenly, discovering whether Robert Blair was her father or not had become unimportant. Finding out about Sarah Tarrant, that was different. Her grandmother was the one she would have loved to know.

'Now, let's talk about you, Serenity. Tell me about the man you're going to marry. Have you been in touch with him about the ring? I'm sure he was very upset.'

'He's overseas . . .' She stopped and looked at Cam. Yes, she could trust him, and she needed someone to talk to. 'If I tell you something about myself, will you regard it as confidential?'

'I'm in that line of business,' Cam said with an encouraging smile.

'Of course, I'd forgotten, only it's hard to know where to start. I feel so guilty, yet I haven't really told any lies.' She paused to marshal her thoughts. 'I'm not getting married. There is no fiancé.'

'Tell me about it.' Cam's eyes were very understanding.

It all came tumbling out, about her mother dying, about John, about Mrs Bellamy, and about her father's appearance and his announcement. Naturally she didn't mention the photo or that her mother came from this district. Nor did she say anything about falling in love with Hudson. Some things she wouldn't share with anyone.

Cam heard her out in silence, then said thoughtfully, 'I can see you've been through a fairly rough patch, and I think you handled it remarkably well. You don't seem to have held any resentment or even bitterness towards your father or towards John. I'm glad of that. Hate and anger held in the heart can destroy a person; you are free of that. I don't even detect any self-pity, and you've every reason to feel hard done by. So tell me why you

feel guilty. I can't for the life of me see your problem.'

'It's Hudson. It's the ring,' Serenity said desperately.
'You see, I told you about the wedding dress, and
Hudson saw it, and saw the ring, and I let him go on
thinking I was getting married. It seemed the best way at
the time, but now it's as if I were living a lie. I do feel
badly about it.'

'You haven't told him any lies, presumably, so you're
in the clear. If you didn't want to confide the whole story
in him when you arrived, that's understandable. If it
really worries you, tell him now. He's a fine chap,
Hudson. He'd be understanding, sympathetic, in fact.'

'You're joking. He'd be furious. He asked me several
times if I still loved John, and I assured him I did. Well, I
do, as I told you, but not the marrying kind of love.'

'Definitely not, and in my opinion, it never was.
You've had a lucky escape. Being sorry for a man is no
reason for marrying him.'

'I know that now,' Serenity wailed. 'But don't you see,
Hudson would not have asked me to stay if I hadn't been
engaged to John. Look, it was really important to him.'

'Yes, I can see that he made a real thing about it. I
don't really see why, except that he was trying to protect
himself a little. Girls rather tend to throw themselves at
him, and I suppose he didn't want that happening, not
when you're sharing the same house. That's pretty close
quarters to dodge about in. Then again, he was probably
making sure you were also protected. Having a fiancé,
and planning a wedding soon, would scotch any local
gossip about him having such a young, pretty housekeeper.'

Serenity kept quiet, but watched him hopefully. If he
said the best thing was to admit it and leave, she would
take his advice.

'It's funny, Hudson is usually well able to take care of himself in any situation, and he's not worried about gossipmongers. Perhaps it was for Madeline's benefit.'

'It would take more than me to upset Madeline Buchanan.'

'You're right. My advice is to let things ride. You're enjoying yourself here. You seem to have a really good relationship with Hudson. I've been watching the two of you this past week, and I've never seen him looking more relaxed. I can't see how you can leave with all this kerfuffle about the ring going on.'

'Yes, there's still the ring. I'm really upset about losing it. I feel responsible for all this bother, yet I'm not devastated by its loss. I want to find it, and return it to John; then I'll feel free to start my life again. Until I find it, I somehow feel tied to John, beholden to him. Does that sound silly?'

'No, I can understand that. If you don't find it, you're going to get entangled in arguments over the insurance, and it will bring you back in contact with him, and you don't want that.'

'So you don't think it's dishonest to stay under these circumstances? I'd like to stay. It's only for another four weeks.'

'A lot can happen in four weeks,' Cam said with a frown. 'Don't get caught on the rebound. Hudson is a very attractive man, and he's got quite a reputation with women. Don't get hurt, Serenity. He's a hard man. If you find yourself becoming attracted, pack your bags and leave.'

Serenity looked at the floor, her dark lashes fanning her pale cheeks, and sighed.

'Oh, Serenity, you poor kid.' Cam touched her hand. Get out while the going is good. If he finds out the truth about your engagement, he'll consider you fair game. If you're already in love with him, your resistance will be a token gesture. Don't risk it. I'm warning you that the crisis you're in now will pale in significance compared with what will happen if you let him use you, then reject you.'

'I'm stronger than you think.' Serenity's chin came up.

'Not that strong, Serenity, none of us is. Still, it's your decision, and I'll be about the place. Come and talk to me any time. I'm your friend, remember that.'

'Yes, I will. And thanks for listening. You've lived here all your life, Cam. Did you know the girl Hudson was going to marry? The one he built this house for?'

'Yes, I did. She was my cousin, and they met when she was over visiting at our place. It was love at first sight. She was a very sweet, gentle girl, and Hudson, he was different then, more kind, more sensitive. It was a sad thing to happen.'

'He told me she died. How did she die? Or is that prying?'

'Not at all. She died of leukaemia, and it was fairly fast. Well, they didn't find out she had it until six months before she died. This house was built . . .'

'But he is so bitter?' Serenity made it a question.

Cam was silent for a few moments. 'Well, considering the circumstances, I'll tell you what happened. It might make you understand him a little better. He's a great chap, Hudson, but he really let this eat into him. Not her death, he could have handled that, but Emma didn't give him that chance. When she found out what she had, she kept it a secret from him. She just broke off the engagement, no explanation. He nearly went crazy, because he loved her. He must have worn out a set of tyres, driving over the hill and back to see her, pleading with her, trying to find out why she had changed her mind. She lived in Canterbury. It went on for about a month, then she told him she had another man, and she backed it up by being seen with him.'

'Why did she do it?' Serenity asked in shocked tones.

'God only knows why she did it. She crippled him, but she thought she was doing the right thing. She loved him so much, she said, she didn't want him to see her ugly and in pain. She thought it would be easier on him to remember her as she was, but it was sheer stupidity. He was finally convinced that she loved this other chap, and he cleared out overseas for a year. He came back a changed man, harder, tougher, even cruel as far as women are concerned.'

'When did he find out that she had leukaemia?'

'After she died. She'd left a letter for him. It made no difference—her explanation—not as far as I could see. The rejection had taken all the stuffing out of him, then the letter must have made him feel that she counted his love as a pretty small thing, if she would not let him stand by her at such a time.'

'How terrible. Poor Hudson, no wonder he's hard.'

'Yes, and it needn't have happened. I know about it now only because Emma was family. I heard it at the funeral and it snarled me up for a while, because I liked them both so much. It's not common knowledge. Oh, the house and the broken engagement were, he had to wear that publicly, but the rest, not many know. Hudson will never talk about it. I know that, because I've tried. I know his parents have tried, and others, but it's like trying to get through a wall of solid cement.'

'The hurt must have gone very deep,' Serenity said sadly.

'Yes, it did, but don't let your sympathy overcome your caution, as far as Hudson's concerned. I'll give you a hand with these dishes, and then I'll get home. I've got to preach in the morning.'

'You do? Where?'

'Down at the schoolhouse. They have a service there once a month. Get Hudson to bring you, ten o'clock. Everyone turns up; you'll meet the whole district there.'

Serenity started to clear the table. 'Does Hudson always go?'

'Yes, of course. Even he can sit for one hour a month, and he's very community minded. There'll be the Vicar from Ahaura, to see I don't step out of line.' His eyes were smiling and very blue.

'I'll come,' Serenity promised. 'Does Miss Buchanan turn out?'

Cam hung up the teatowel. 'No. She hasn't honoured us with her presence yet, but when she and Hudson are married, I'm sure she'll do the correct thing. She probably won't rise till midday, tomorrow.'

'You're sure they'll marry?'

'Pretty sure, and they are well suited.'

Serenity walked to the Utility with him. 'I don't agree; she is hard. I'd say ruthless.'

'My opinion exactly,' Cam said. 'They'll be very suitable partners.'

Serenity opened her mouth to protest, then closed it again. She waved Cam away, then went to sit on the patio under the stars. Cam was wrong, there was a different sort of hardness in Madeline. She was diamond hard, and diamonds could mutilate glass and drill through steel . . . She knew Hudson was different.

She also knew Cam's advice was good, that she should go upstairs and pack her bags. She was going to be hurt otherwise. How had Hudson described the river in flood? 'A raging torrent, carrying everything before it.' Well, that's how she felt. She was in the grip of something much more powerful than herself, and if it was sweeping her to destruction, it was too late to get away.

CHAPTER SIX

SLEEP eluded Serenity entirely, but she lay on her bed resting, looking oot her window at the myriads of stars, enthralled with their beauty, and the silver-and-white glory of the Alps. She had this whole vast valley to herself and she revelled in it. She was picking up small pieces of knowledge that she would keep when she left. The highest peak was Mount Elizabeth, and somewhere beyond that was the beautiful Lake Morgan where the deerstalkers went to shoot deer. She knew the name of Brian O'Lynn, the mountain which towered above the house.

She went over in her mind the story of Emma, the girl who had loved Hudson, who had this house built for her, who had been loved by Hudson, and who died before she could enjoy any of it. She could empathise with her. To be full of health and life and beauty, and to know she was going to lose it all, would have been hard enough, but to have Hudson watch the deterioration would have been terrible.

Who could blame her for wanting to shut herself away? Yet how could she have hurt Hudson so much? Surely there must have been another way. She didn't need to destroy his love completely. If only she had not introduced the other man. But then she must have been desperate, to be losing her strength, and scared to be losing her resolve to do what she had to do alone. Serenity's heart ached for her.

Emma had loved Hudson with all her heart, yet she had felt it necessary to send him away. It had been her way of showing love. And Hudson would not be a man to be put off easily. He would have persisted, persevered. Cam had said he had worn out a set of tyres . . . how many trips over the mountains did it take to do that? How many miles? How many hours? And each visit must have been agony for her, turning him away, when she must have longed for the comfort and strength of his love to support her.

But Emma had held to her purpose and Serenity could only admire her for having the courage of her convictions, yet she had been so wrong. In trying to spare Hudson from the pain of watching her die, she had served him a worse hurt. She had crushed his spirit, and made him wary of ever trusting or loving a woman again. The price had been too high.

Serenity felt the tears pouring down her cheeks, and rolled over to bury her head in her pillow. Emma had missed her chance, and she had also effectively wiped out any hope Serenity had of reaching Hudson. She loved him, but she could never tell him so. Cam was right. Hudson would marry Madeline, and somehow at this moment Serenity did not envy her. Madeline would never know that she had only half a man, that he would keep the best part of himself separate from her, that his heart was like a sealed unit, denying entrance to love.

She must have fallen asleep in the early hours, only to be woken by loud voices from the patio below.

'I'm only warning you for your own good, Hudson.'

'I don't need your guidance in this matter, Madeline. You have already bored me to tears with the subject. I don't tell you how to handle your court briefs. I resent your trying to interfere in the running of the Bar 2. I'll hire whom I like, when I like, and now let's drop the whole discussion. I'm tired.'

'You don't know *one* thing about this girl, Hudson. I didn't like her . . .'

'She wasn't all that enamoured with you either, but she didn't tell me to get rid of you,' Hudson said harshly. 'You don't own me, Madeline, and even if we marry, you still won't. Don't push me too far, I'm not in the mood. Let's go to bed.'

'If you think I'm sleeping with you with her in the house, you've got another think coming. What do you mean by putting her in my room? What's wrong with the downstairs room? That's where Mrs Batts slept.'

'And I have explained this *ad nauseam*. Batty may just come back, and I wanted her room free. Drop it, will you?'

'Huh! I can read you like a book, Hudson. You wanted her nice and handy . . . upstairs, close to you, when you pulled your big seduction scene. Or have you done that already? You didn't expect me this week-end.'

'Serenity is a decent girl, and you watch your mouth. She is engaged and will be married in six weeks. She's quite safe under my roof. I've never been so short of my basic needs that I had to poach on another man's territory. And I'm still a free agent, as you are. I don't ask what you're up to in Christchurch, but I've heard a few rumours. If we decide to marry I will be faithful to you, and will expect fidelity in return . . .'

'Yes, I know that, Hudson.' Madeline's tone was more conciliatory. 'And I'm sorry about this scene. I wouldn't speak out unless I was truly concerned. You know I haven't protested before, but this girl is different. I feel very suspicious of her. You don't come in contact with the seamy side of life as I do in the city. You get a sixth sense about people—its an instinct. She's false . . .'

'Rubbish. I'd stake my reputation on her honesty,' Hudson shouted angrily.

'That's exactly what I mean. I've never heard you go out on a limb for any woman all the time I've known you. She's got her hooks into you and you're blind to it. You fool! You'll find yourself fronting up to a paternity suit or worse.'

'Chance would be a fine thing,' Hudson answered with a laugh. 'You don't know Serenity.'

'No. Well, I tell you there's something wrong. I bet she hasn't even lost that ring. She's hidden it so she'll have an excuse to stay here. Then the stones may not have been genuine, just paste; they can look very effective. You've swallowed her story hook, line, and sinker, but I haven't. I *will* find out about her, and I *will* be proved correct.'

'So, she pulled a line on you and you probably asked for it. I have always admired your judgment of people, Madeline, but you're wrong about Serenity. I'm sick of the whole thing. She's not important to me, or to you, or to our plans. She has her life, we have ours. Let's drop it.'

'You go to Hell! I'm sleeping downstairs tonight.'

Serenity was sitting up in bed wide-eyed. She heard a door slam viciously downstairs and then silence. Much later she heard Hudson come up to his room and all was quiet.

She lay still waiting for the dawn. She wasn't shocked. She had known that some woman had been a frequent visitor when she had first used that bathroom. Well, she had no illusions now about their relationship or their intention to marry. Nor yet Hudson's view of her. She wasn't important to him, but he did trust her. That was nice. What if he found out about the cancelled wedding? He would think she had lied all the time.

She hated any form of deceit. She'd face him with it tomorrow. After church, after Madeline had left, she would sit down and tell him. She couldn't bear to have him lose his good opinion of her. Serenity knew he would tell her to leave, and it was better that way. She wasn't important to him, and never would be. He had warned her from the start that he didn't want any complications in his life, and she had boasted that he would never become that in hers.

She loved him, and it was like pain and happiness equally mingled; sorrow and joy. If she left now it would just be a memory to treasure, but if she was by his side for four weeks, the love would develop and be harder to recover from. Madeline had done her a favour by arriving at this point in time. Fancy her saying that Serenity had just hidden the ring, or that it was only paste jewellery. What a nasty suspicious mind she had.

And the way they had yelled at each other, they hadn't even cared if they woke her up. She would be well out of it. But she would always be glad that she had come, because of Sarah Tarrant. That house and garden would stay evergreen in her memory. And the ride up river, and the horses, and Cam, and the shearers, gave her plenty of happy times to remember.

The sun shining full on her face woke her from heavy sleep, and she realised it must be very late. Quickly and quietly she washed and dressed and tiptoed downstairs, not wanting to disturb a sleeping household. It was late but she still had time for a cup of tea and get to church on time. She would borrow the Subaru. Hudson wouldn't mind.

'Good morning, Serenity. Did you sleep well?' He was fully dressed in well-cut slacks and elegant shirt and matching tie, looking extremely handsome and very alert.

'Oh, good morning to you both,' Serenity stopped in
surprise. Even Madeline had risen, but she was still
wearing a housecoat.

'You two have met, I gather.' His lips curved in an
amused smile.

'That's true,' Serenity walked forward, glad that she
was wearing her most attractive blue dress and high
heeled shoes. It made her feel more in command of the
situation.

Madeline surveyed her through narrowed eyes.
'Where did you say you came from, Serenity?'

'I didn't,' Serenity said blandly, then shooting a glance
at Hudson asked, 'Is that tea hot?'

'Freshly made, help yourself. I see you're all dolled up
in your Sunday best. I presume Cam warned you church
was at ten. You are coming with me?'

'Love to. I'll take my tea out on the patio, it's a shame
to waste all this sunshine.'

She breathed a sigh of relief as she sat down in the hot
sun. It was so peaceful looking down towards the lake.
Hudson had told her Haupiri, in Maori, meant hidden or
stealthy wind. That was just like her love for him,
hidden, and it had sneaked up on her so stealthily. There
was nothing hidden about Madeline's dislike for her,
that unrelenting stare had followed her every move and
Serenity was sure it was only Hudson's presence which
had saved her from the inquisition. What a beautiful day
it was. When would Madeline leave? She hoped Cam
was given to lengthy sermons.

'Ready, Paleface?' Hudson joined her, his glance
warm and friendly. 'No, don't jump up. Finish your tea
first, we've tons of time. Cam look after you okay last
night?'

'Yes, he was very kind.' In spite of having herself well
under control, she blushed when his knee accidently

touched hers. 'I'll just run up and get my purse and gloves.'

'You do that.' His eyes were lit with mocking laughter as if he knew that she was nervous of him.

She stayed in her room until she was calm again. How gauche and young she must have appeared to him compared with the sophisticated elegance of Madeline. She glared at herself in the mirror. Starry-eyed, that's how Cam had described her. Yes, she looked like a girl in love. Well, it was very new to her, and she would get better at hiding it.

Madeline was standing with Hudson when Serenity came back down to the patio. She was strikingly beautiful in the severely-tailored housegown and she knew it.

'I didn't think you'd risk the sun this early in the day, Madeline,' Hudson said teasingly, but there was a hint of frost in the remark.

'I'm not staying here. I'm off back to bed—I've got a blinding headache.'

'Sorry about that. Hangovers can be miserable whether they are caused by an excess of alcohol, or an excess of emotion. Will I find you an aspirin?'

Serenity went quickly past them and out the gate. So they were still fighting. She didn't mind as long as they didn't make her the meat in the sandwich.

'We'll take the car.' He caught up with her and walked towards the vehicle, tall and tanned, the sun striking his auburn hair making it glow like fire. He held the door for her.

She slid under his arm avoiding his touch and he grinned and slammed the door. She swallowed with difficulty, her mouth was very dry. As he took his place beside her, she asked, 'Does everyone in the district come?'

He gave her a penetrating stare, 'Of course, that's why

you're glowing with excitement. You might find this mysterious patient of yours. You're still not going to give me any clues to help you track him down.'

She smiled brightly as she clicked her safety belt shut. So he thought her excitement was caused by the thought of meeting the people of the district. How convenient. 'No, I won't do that, but I'm pleased you're going with me, you can tell me all the names.'

'Did you get home safely after I left you last night?' he flicked a meaningful glance towards her as he drove off.

'Of course.' She met his look without flinching. He was trying to embarrass her, well two could play at that game. 'You couldn't have got much sleep yourself last night? I heard you come in.'

Hudson concentrated on his driving, and Serenity relaxed a little. She was becoming very familiar with this drive to the main road and was grateful for the cattle-stops. At least she didn't have to leap out five times on the way down. Only the main road gate had to be opened.

She hurried to fling it back and her heart lifted and soared as his face creased into that special smile he had for her. Native birds filled the air with throbbing music, and wild ducks flapped frantically from the deep black stream. Was being in love always like this? The sun warmer and more brilliant, the bush, the flax and the fern, the waving toi toi fronds, each took on a shape and beauty of such intensity that she ached with the splendour of it all.

And beyond the physical pain was the pulsating joy of loving Hudson. Just to sit beside him in the car, to watch the shade and shadow of the trees touch his face, made her bones melt.

He stopped on the Bluff overlooking the Station, his gaze searching for some sheep or cattle below, and she watched him, trying to memorise every detail of his face. Today she was close to him, she could touch him if she wanted to, she would sit by him in church, be introduced to his neighbours by him, and tomorrow she would be gone.

Had her mother felt like this? Had her mother's love for her man been of the same magnitude? And she had walked away, not only leaving him but this valley, and her own mother. Everything she had held dear, and she must have been just Serenity's age. What was that song she used to sing? 'It's the hard times that make you strong.' Her mother had an inner strength, a belief that there was a higher power, a God who cared for her personally. Serenity needed that too.

'Here we are, and we're just in time. Jump to it. You could at least wait till you get inside to go back to sleep.'

Serenity gave him a reproachful look as she got out. 'I wasn't asleep,' she protested as he caught her up and taking her arm led her into the small school house set in a bush clearing.

Cam saw them and nodded a greeting. A strangely different Cam, wearing a suit with a surplice over it, yet he looked marvellous; his face seemed to shine as bright as his gold hair.

There were only fifteen or twenty people in the whole room, even counting the children. Most of them turned to greet Hudson and to look at her with frank curiosity. Then as she stood for the first hymn she saw Cam's father with his family.

There was no doubt in her mind that he was the man in the photo, older now, but very distinguished, and still handsome. As she watched he must have felt her gaze because he turned and saw her. Her heart somersaulted and her voice wobbled off key as his penetrating blue eyes held hers in shock and amazement. She saw him pale as if seeing a ghost and then he turned again to the front, squaring his shoulders as if to set himself for what might come.

Was she so like her mother? Had she unconsciously dressed for this meeting? Wearing a plain blue dress with pearl buttons down the front and a neat white Peter Pan collar, a simple style which could have been worn ten, twenty, thirty years ago. And she'd worn her fair hair loose and flowing smoothly over her shoulders. She hadn't meant to create an image, but if she had done it deliberately, it couldn't have been done better.

Serenity didn't hear much of the service. She wished she could leave, but she had asked Hudson to introduce her to everyone. He would think it strange if she suddenly developed a headache and fled to the safety of the car. Worse, he would suspect she had found her target and would question her adroitly until the secret was out.

She looked at Cam's mother and the two teenage boys, and wished with all her heart that she had not come. Would Robert Blair speak to her? Would he *challenge* her? He wouldn't know that she had no intention of bringing up the past. She was a threat to him, and he didn't look like a man who would scare easily.

She forced herself to listen to Cam, and caught the tail end of his sermon. 'Love does not act unbecomingly, it does not seek its own way, does not take into account a wrong suffered, is not provoked. Love never fails.'

They rose for the last hymn, and as they filed out, they shook hands with the Vicar and Cam and moved into the bright sunlight.

Cam followed them. 'Glad you could both come. Serenity, I want you to meet my family.'

'She'll meet everyone, Cam, that's what she wants.' Hudson took her arm with such a proprietorial air that if it had happened anywhere else she would have been in her seventh heaven. As it was she used it as a prop, drawing comfort and strength from his presence. As he took her from group to group, she kept looking to the door, knowing that the Blairs would be last out, hoping that Robert Blair would go straight for his car.

Then she saw Cam leading them towards her and her fingers clutched Hudson's arm too tightly, communicating her fear.

'Are you okay, Serenity?' he demanded with concern in his voice.

'Of course. It was a bit hot in there with the sun streaming through the windows, but it's lovely out here.'

He nodded, satisfied because others had been complaining about the same thing. 'Morning Robert, Mrs Blair. Nice day. I'd like you to meet Serenity James who is staying with me at present.'

Mrs Blair took Serenity's hand in both hers. 'Cam has told us so much about you, my dear. It's a pleasure to meet you. He said you'd managed marvellously well cooking for the shearers. The first time is always the worst. I flinch when I think of the mistakes I made. Oh, my dear, I was so sorry to hear about the loss of your ring. But it will turn up. I was saying to Cam, there's more than gold and diamonds in a betrothal ring. It's a symbol of the love of a man for his future wife, and God will bring it back to you.'

'I do hope so,' Serenity managed, so very conscious of the tall silver-haired man waiting his turn to meet her. Why didn't he go!

Cam's mother rattled on happily, blissfully unaware of the tension building up between the two people on either side of her. Serenity thought she was lovely but wished she would be quiet so that the ordeal could be over. She glanced up at Robert Blair and saw the same thought reflected in his eyes. As their gaze locked she knew why Robert Blair had not left, he was not a man who had ever run away from anything in his life. Incredibly, the strain left his face and he smiled at her, and she smiled back. A weight of worry rolled away and she felt lightheaded with relief. In that moment they had communicated and understood each other without one word being spoken. He knew her, and he knew also that she was not there to cause trouble.

Mrs Blair chattered on, 'Why, Robert will tell you, I was nearly distraught when I lost my engagement ring, when the boys were small. They had used it for a hunt the thimble game, and it was missing for years. I wouldn't let Robert replace it. It's not the same at all, you do understand. And where do you think it turned up? Wadded in tissue paper and thrust into a bedroom door lock. It had been so close to me all the time. One day at lunch, Cam, for no reason at all, walked over to the door and pried it loose. Oh, I can tell you we had a celebration that day.'

At last she was quiet and Robert Blair held out his hand, and enveloping Serenity's small one in a bone-crushing grip, said warmly, 'It's a genuine pleasure to meet you, Miss Serenity James. I've been standing here watching you. You remind me of someone I knew years ago. The resemblance is uncanny. She was a beautiful girl and a very dear friend of mine. I couldn't pay you a greater compliment than to compare you with her.'

'I've been wanting to meet you, too.' Serenity's eyes were soft and brilliant. 'Because you're Cam's father and he has talked so much about you.'

He smiled with complete understanding. 'Yes, he does go on a bit. If you're staying in the district for a while Cam must bring you up for dinner one night.'

'I'd love that,' Serenity said happily, but she knew that it would not happen. Straight after lunch she would talk to Hudson and then she would leave. This visit had filled in so many blanks in her life. She knew that she and Robert Blair would never discuss the past. She didn't want to know the details. She never had, only to be assured that he had loved her mother and she had that assurance now.

'Not just for a meal, come for the weekend,' Mrs Blair had protested. 'Cam, you bring her. In this all-male household I get so lonely for feminine company.'

Cam laughed, 'I don't think I'll do that. While she's at Hudson's I do get a chance to talk to her. If I bring her home you'd monopolise the conversation.'

Everyone else had drifted off and as Serenity walked to the car her feet hardly touched the ground. Robert Blair could have come straight out and said Sarah Tarrant was her grandmother, but he hadn't. She was so happy, so blissfully happy.

Hudson held the car door for her, 'I must say you've revived remarkably well. You look as if you've won a million dollars.' He strode around the car and took his seat. 'Did you find your elusive patient?'

'Yes, I did, that's why I'm so happy,' she informed him with a contented sigh.

He switched on the motor, then gave her smiling face a puzzled scrutiny. 'I listened to every word you said, and yet I must have missed something.'

'Oh, you certainly did,' Serenity's laugh was full of delight. 'And I'm not going to satisfy your curiosity. I told you it was very confidential.'

She snuggled back in her seat. Should she get him to stop on the way home and give it to him straight? He would be very angry. But at least she would have it off her conscience. And it would stop Madeline giving her the third degree over lunch. What were those words in the service which had reminded her of Madeline? 'That they may truly and indifferently minister justice to the punishment of wickedness and vice.' Yes, she could just see Madeline dishing out a load of indifferent justice to her if she had the opportunity.

'Madeline is leaving for Christchurch straight after lunch, and we'll go over the other side. Terry Goulder is coming with his scanner. Perhaps today you'll have your ring back.'

'I hope so.' They were nearly home. She was glad she hadn't talked to him. She would much rather wait until Madeline had gone. She could imagine Madeline's delight at being proved right that Serenity may have told the truth but not the whole truth.

'Good, there's Tessa and Lee and the kids home. I'm glad they're back. We'll give them time to unpack, then call and see them. Would you like to drive round this afternoon or ride across?'

'Oh, ride the river, any time.' Her face lit with enthusiasm.

'My sentiments exactly.' He braked in front of the house. 'Hop in and put some lunch on. Nothing fancy, lettuce salad and open a tin of meat.'

'What would your previous housekeeper have served you for lunch?' Serenity demanded.

'Oh, Colonial goose, gravy, roast potatoes, and all the trimmings,' Hudson said cheerfully.

'She must have spoiled you terribly. You must miss her a lot.'

'Not as much as I expected to.' His hazel eyes sparkled with mischief.

As she unclipped her safety belt, he touched her shoulder. 'As a favour to me, keep the peace in there, will you? I hate friction. And we'll be on our own again in about an hour or so.'

Serenity smiled at him, 'Okay, Boss, whatever you

say.' She was too happy to quarrel with anyone, even Madeline.

'That's my girl,' he winked at her and drove towards the garage.

She walked up the path with music all around her. His girl: So what if it was only an expression, casually used. It was a nice one. And he had said they would be on their own in a couple of hours, as if the idea pleased him as much as it did her.

When she walked in she stared at the dining-room table. What a surprise! It was set to perfection; an elegant embossed table cloth with matching napkins, handsome heavy silverware, glistening crystal glasses, and a fabulous dinner set, of fine imported china. An intricate arrangement of flowers sat in the centrepiece and carefully placed about were bowls of crisp salad, tomato flowers on beds of lettuce, cucumber rings with fluted edges, beetroot, and grated cheese, also fresh celery stalks.

'If you want to freshen up, Serenity, lunch is almost ready.'

Serenity swivelled around to find Madeline smiling at her. She really knew how to dress. Her outfit would have graced the cover of Vogue magazine without a blush.

'Yes, I'll do that. The table looks fantastic. You must have worked very hard while we've been away.'

'It's no more trouble to do things correctly than it is just to throw things together. If you know *how* to do it, of course.'

Serenity's eyes flashed. She had offered her a genuine compliment. But Hudson had said to keep the peace, so she quietly went to her room. Freshen up indeed! Madeline had made her feel like a country clodhopper, and she had meant to. And that gleam of barely concealed triumph behind her smile, was it because of the lunch table? If so, she was rightly entitled to it. She must have really thrown herself into it.

But Serenity thought that behind the smile there was more than ordinary pleasure at up-marketing her with a meal. Her ladyship had looked too smug for good health, Serenity's health. But she, Serenity, had spent the morning with Hudson. It would take a lot to top that.

She tidied herself and went down to the lounge to wait for Hudson. When he came up the path he was whistling *her* tune, and her mouth curved in a delighted smile.

Madeline leaned up to kiss him. 'You sound very cheerful, Hudson. Isn't it a glorious day? The wine is ready, if you'll do the honours, darling. Sorry, if I was a little beastly last night, I'd had a very tough week in court. I'd like your advice on one of the cases as we have lunch.'

'Sure, where's the wine?' He surveyed the table. 'You've done magnificently, Madeline.'

She handed him the wine. 'I'll get the garlic bread from the oven, you do enjoy it so much. It's good that you can appreciate the little extra effort I've taken. Any meal is so much more enjoyable when presented properly.'

Serenity sat quiet and thoughtful. Full marks to her ladyship, with her charming apology. Hudson was obviously pleased by it, and the attention he was receiving. Any red-blooded male would be flattered by such a display of charm and affection. These two obviously understood each other. Cam was right—they were a perfect match.

'Come along, Serenity. Do join us, don't feel shy,' Madeline purred.

Serenity took her place with some misgiving.

'Shrimp cocktail, Hudson, your favourite, and I've

made that very *special* sauce, darling. Serenity, my dear, I didn't mean to confuse you with the array of cutlery. You use that one. And beware of the pâté. You are used to good plain fare, and I wouldn't like to upset your digestion.'

Serenity gritted her teeth. Something was upsetting her digestion, but it wasn't the pâté. She glared across at Hudson. If he wanted peace he had better tame that tigress sitting beside him.

He met her gaze with a conspiratorial wink. 'We've been to church, learning about loving our neighbour, haven't we, Serenity?'

Somewhat mollified, Serenity accepted the wine from him. Let Madeline have her fun, she would be gone soon. Anyway she was using the wrong tactics. Men always leaned towards the underdogs in a battle.

Madeline then effectively cut Serenity out of the conversation by relating at length to Hudson her problem with a certain case that was continuing next week in court. There was no doubt that she had a fine intelligent mind, and the topic had been chosen carefully as one that would hold Hudson's attention.

By the coffee stage, Serenity wished she could leave them to get on with it, but good manners made her sit there patiently.

Suddenly Madeline turned her attention to Serenity. 'Now, tell me all about your wedding. When exactly are you getting married?'

'When John gets back.'

'You mean you haven't got a date set?' Her eyes widened in disbelief. 'I thought it took ages to arrange a wedding.'

'Not always,' Serenity said quietly. 'When John gets back we'll discuss it.'

'How romantic. What a shame you couldn't have

travelled with him overseas. It would have been a great honeymoon under the tropical skies.'

'Yes, it would have been,' Serenity's eyes narrowed. Madeline was pushing for some sort of victory.

'That gorgeous dress hanging in the wardrobe. I was quite envious when I saw the designer's name. Did you choose it yourself? It shows excellent taste, and I must congratulate you.'

Fancy her snooping through the room! At least her case was locked. She couldn't have had much time, being fairly well occupied with this lunch. Still, keep the peace.

'John's mother chose the dress, I'll pass your congratulations on.'

'How very charming. She must be pleased to have you join the family if she helped you choose such a fabulous gown. Was she pleased with the engagement?'

Serenity scented danger. 'Not exactly, but then John is an only child, so some allowances must be made.'

'And your own parents. They would be pleased for you I'm sure.'

Serenity felt like a biological specimen under a microscope, and she knew now this wasn't a casual chat. Madeline's eyes telegraphed that she was closing in for the kill.

'My mother is dead. Look I'd rather not talk about the wedding. It was postponed and I find it somewhat painful . . .'

Madeline rose gracefully, but her eyes glittered like an eagle about to swoop on its prey. 'I'm sure you must find it very painful. After all, there isn't going to be a wedding, is there, Serenity? You and John are not going to be married. He has broken off his engagement to you and to get out of your reach was forced to travel overseas. And you're not entitled to the ring that you've so carelessly lost. You kept it even after the family asked for it back. You're no better than a thief.'

'That's not true . . .' Serenity was also on her feet, her face pale under the attack.

'Nothing's true, is it, Serenity? You aren't an orphan. Your father is some drunkard who gatecrashed . . .'

'Stop it, stop it. You're twisting everything about.'

'You wouldn't know the truth if you fell over it. You have come here under false pretences. You have fed Hudson an orchestrated litany of lies, to coin Judge Mahon's words, and he, more fool, believed you.'

'I did not tell him one single lie,' Serenity protested. 'Where did you get all this garbage?'

'I'll tell you. The truth will out, Serenity. It just dropped into my lap, or ear rather. A jeweller from up North rang just after you'd left. Something about insurance on the ring. I took the call, and to do you a favour rang Mrs Bellamy to pass on the good news. When she heard the story you were telling she ridiculed it out of hand, a tissue of lies from start to finish. Ask her, Hudson, your so-honest, George Washington-style housekeeper. Is she going to marry John Bellamy?'

Hudson also stood up. 'Yes, Serenity, I would like to hear you repeat the fact that you are still going to marry John.'

'I will not repeat it, because I have never said it to you like that. I said John wanted to marry me, and that is . . .'

'Be quiet! You're a liar and a cheat, and I'm bitterly disappointed in you.' Hudson cut her off.

She looked at his harsh, forbidding face. It was no use. That was the one question he had never asked her. If he had she would have told him the truth. Why hadn't she talked to him on the way home? Dear God, help me, she prayed deep within herself. She really didn't deserve this. How Mrs Bellamy must have gloated? And Madeline had lapped it up.

'Go to your room and pack your bags, Miss James,' Madeline ordered coldly. 'I'm leaving for Christchurch immediately. It will give me great pleasure to escort you off the premises.' She turned to Hudson. 'It's the least I can do for you, darling. I did warn you, but then you're not as used to this type of girl as I am.'

Serenity felt sick. It would serve Madeline right if she was ill all over her elegant table setting. She wouldn't cry. Dry-eyed, she faced Hudson across the table, waiting for his verdict.

'No, Madeline. I'll clean up my own mistakes. I'm grateful to you for sorting this thing out, but I'd like you to leave now. I'll see you out to your car.'

'I'm not leaving while this girl is still here. I demand that you send her packing.'

'You will leave, Madeline, and immediately. You're not yet in the position to demand anything from me. I've already said I'm grateful, you'll have to be satisfied with that. I don't like to be on the receiving end of a confidence trick, and I have every intention of making Miss James regret the day she chose me for her mark. We'll go over to the Homestead now, the chap with the scanner will be waiting. With luck we'll have the ring back tonight, and it will be returned to the Bellamy family. That should take care of one problem.'

'You don't *need* her for that, Hudson.'

'I know that. But if the ring is not found I have to take her to the Police Station tomorrow to make an official statement of loss, and I will be standing by to see that she gives them the correct story. She also has to be taken to the insurance company to complete formalities concerning her car and receive her cheque.'

'Hudson, she can do all these things in Christchurch. I

guarantee that I will see that she does them.'

'Furthermore,' he continued harshly as if Madeline had not spoken, 'I made a deal with Miss James and when I make a deal it stands. She will stay here and work her passage for four weeks, there's no telling what a little hard labour might do to her character. And I'll bet even money she'll regret each and every day she spends here.'

'I won't stay,' Serenity cried passionately. 'You can't make me stay.'

'I wouldn't count on that.' The look from his hazel eyes sharpened dangerously. 'You agreed you would stay. You gave me your word on it. Is that a fact?'

'Yes, but circumstances have changed. I'd rather starve than work for you.'

'Yours might have, but mine haven't. I still need a housekeeper. You were the one talking so loudly last night about being committed to a project. Well, I'm giving you a chance to prove your words. For once in your life make an honest effort to fulfil a contract. Who knows, it might be the turning point in your life. You might even enjoy going straight.' He was bitingly sarcastic.

'Right, I will, and I won't be the only one who's sorry. I will get John to come down here and tell you the truth. He'll tell you he still wants to marry me, and that he begged me to go on wearing his ring. He wants the wedding to go ahead. I was the one who changed my mind. You'll apologise one day for treating me this way.'

'I wouldn't hold my breath, if I were you. I am sure it's entirely possible that you could twist that besotted young man around your finger, and even bring him down here to confirm your outrageous lies. I said you were a cool customer, Serenity James, but you've gone even further than I would have predicted. The deal is on then, you're staying.'

'Yes, I'll stay,' Serenity said threateningly. 'Remember it was at your request.'

'I'll remember. Now clear this table off and look smart about it. I'll see Miss Buchanan out, then catch the horses, and you'd better be ready when I shout.'

'Aren't you going to count the silver before I touch it, or do you prefer to frisk me when I leave?'

Ignoring her, he shepherded the still very voluble Madeline out to her car. Serenity sat down weakly on a chair. If only she had talked to him on the way home. They had been friends then, he would have believed her. What had she done by agreeing to stay? He would never change his mind about her because he thought she was a liar and a cheat.

Almost blinded by tears she started to clear the lunch things away. What had Cam said? 'If he ever finds out about the engagement being off, you'd better watch it. He will look on you as fair game.' She shivered. Was *that* why he was making her stay?

CHAPTER SEVEN

SERENITY had finished the dishes, changed into jeans and casual top, and was waiting at the gate when Hudson stopped with the horses.

'Bring your bikini and a towel, we'll have a quick dip on the way over.'

Serenity hesitated. She would love a swim, because it was boiling hot, but with Hudson in the mood he was in, she preferred to stay hot.

'You don't need to be scared of me,' he jeered as if reading her thoughts. 'I wouldn't touch you with a forty-foot barge-pole.'

She ran through the house fighting back her tears. He needn't be quite so brutal. She stripped off her clothes and put on her bikini, then dressed again, grabbed a towel and a windbreaker and ran out to take her horse.

'Here's your hat. Do you think we should get another colour? White is hardly appropriate.' He threw it at her feet.

She picked it up and swung on to the horse. It didn't matter what he thought of her—she knew she wasn't a liar and a cheat. He hadn't given her Misty today because he didn't want her too close to him. If she fell off in the river, he probably wouldn't even bother to pull her out. Well, she wouldn't drown to satisfy him.

At the river he waved towards the bush. 'You can change over there. Tie your horse securely or you'll walk the rest of the way.'

After slipping out of her clothes, Serenity stood on the bank watching him ploughing his way across the green depths and then plunged in herself. She came up gasping for breath. Cold, it was glacier cold! She struck out for the other side, enjoying having something to fight against. It was a release to do something violently physical, and by the time she had made it back she felt refreshed and invigorated.

She dressed and was ready waiting by the time Hudson reappeared. She crossed the river carefully behind him and was aware that he was choosing much deeper channels for her to negotiate. Perhaps this was the shortest route but she had a feeling that he was deliberately testing her. She wouldn't panic in front of him, she thought grimly, nor would she call out for help, even if she was going down for the third time.

He waited on the edge of the furthermost stream. 'Why can't you keep up?'

She glared back at him. 'I'll swap you horses and see if you can make this one keep up with Rajah.'

He then galloped away and was soon lost from sight. She had no idea where the track was to get off the riverbed and turn in by the cattle yards. She was sure she had not even been in this part of the country the last time she was out with him. Well, there was only one way to go. She slapped the stocky horse into a gallop, saying cheerfully, 'Righto, Dobbin, it's all yours. You take me there.'

Hudson was just leaning down to fasten the gate as she galloped through the small stream in a shower of spray, and as he swung it open for her she saw the gleam in his eye? Was it admiration? He had hoped that she would spend the whole afternoon lost in that wilderness. He didn't intend to do her any favours. She rode through without speaking, her head held high.

Terry Goulder was waiting for them to arrive and only too eager to demonstrate his marvellous machine.

Serenity was fascinated as she saw it sweep the ground and bleep bleep each time it crossed some metal.

'Don't know how it will work inside the woolshed. It's liable to bounce off nails in the walls and floor. Can you rig up something, Hudson? I need a table without metal in it.'

'How about swinging a couple of these bales around and then putting a sheet of hardboard across? Is there any chance you can pick it up if it's actually in the bale?'

'Only if it's near the outside. The scanner will only pick up to a maximum depth of three inches, but we could zoom over them just in case it's near the surface.'

By the time the first bale was tested, Serenity had some idea how long the job was going to take . . . hours and hours, as the scanner was only the size of a tennis racquet. When the table was set up, she followed Terry's instructions and spread the wool from under the shearing board out at a three inch depth and waited anxiously.

As he swept over it suddenly it began to bleep madly and she ran forward and searched the wool, only to come up with a five cent piece. She was utterly downcast.

'That's my test bit,' Terry informed her. 'That's how I can tell if it's really working. There's nothing here, clear this off and get some more.'

Hudson had stood by watching the demonstration. 'Great little gadget that. Put that wool straight into the press, Serenity, save moving it a third time. You carry on here, I'll be back later.'

The scanner was very good, even to picking up a piece of silver paper, and once a broken sliver off a shearer's comb. Each time it bleeped Serenity felt madly excited, then terribly disappointed. Terry kept her interested by telling her all the different things he had found and how he used it hunting for gold. He even gave her a spell with it and she was fascinated, but it was so slow. They had hardly touched the huge mass of wool even after two hours solid work.

'Tell you what, Serenity,' Terry said. 'I won't be using this next week. If you like I'll loan it to you. You can come here in your spare time and go through the rest of it. It will take you ages, but if it's there this wee beauty will search it out. What do you say?'

'I'd be most grateful, and I'd be very careful with it. If I were to tease that wool by hand I'd be here for the rest of my life.'

'It's all yours then. And I do wish you luck. Just drop it in to the Store at the Creek when you're in for the mail. I'll be off then.'

Serenity waved him away and then carried on for another hour before Hudson poked his head in. 'Where's Terry?'

'He had to go home, but he's lent me the scanner for a week. Isn't that great?'

'Great,' Hudson said sourly. 'At the rate you're going you'll need to work night and day for the next month to get through it all. As you're working for me during the day, you can spend your nights here.'

'That'll be a pleasure. It means I won't have to put up with your sarcastic comments, day and night,' Serenity answered tartly. 'Where will I leave this for safety?'

'You've got very security conscious all of a sudden. Pity you hadn't been more careful with Bellamy's ring.'

'My ring,' Serenity corrected him carefully. 'I think I'll hide the scanner under this pile of wool. No one will think of looking for it there. See you don't press it up.'

She stretched her aching back. 'Are we going home now?'

'Yes, get moving. I'm hungry and it's getting dark.' He walked out of the shed with an impatient stride.

Serenity hoisted herself into the saddle dispiritedly. It

was going to be a horrible month, with Hudson snarling at her all the time. At least he wasn't galloping away on her this time. Probably because he'd find it embarrassing explaining how he came to lose a new chum on the riverbed, and not out of any concern for her.

She stumbled with tiredness as she unsaddled her horse and Hudson just stood there, stern and impatient, not offering to help. It had been a long long day, and she felt drained from the emotional upheaval as well as not having any sleep the night before.

She showered and changed into fresh clothes then began to prepare the vegetables for dinner. Hudson had gone through to the lounge and was watching a television programme. Even yesterday he would have helped her prepare the meal, would have made the task lighter by teasing her. But at least the silent treatment was better than his sarcasm.

The phone rang and Hudson answered it. 'One of your admirers,' he snapped at her.

Serenity ran to the phone, 'Hullo.'

'Cameron Blair here. How are you?'

'Fine.'

'What's the matter? You looked wonderful this morning, now you've got all the bounce of a flat tyre. Didn't you find your ring?'

'Oh, that . . .'

'So that's not the reason you're down. Do you want me to have twenty guesses, or are you going to tell me? Remember me? I'm your friend.'

'Oh, Cam . . .' Tears flooded down her cheeks. 'You don't know what a mess I'm in.'

'No, I don't, but I'm going to find out. I'll be over in an hour.'

'I can't ask you to come so far. We haven't even had dinner yet. I'm so tired. I wish I was dead.'

'I'm coming down. You haven't asked me, but I'd like to see you. Would you like to see me?'

There was so much real concern in his voice that she could hardly answer him. 'More than anything else.'

'See you then. Goodbye.'

She returned to the kitchen rubbing her eyes, and started to get the table laid. She ignored Hudson standing grimly looking at her.

'Going to make a play for young Cam now. He's an impressionable chap, but once I let him know what you've been up to you can whistle and he won't come running. He's got honesty too, but not like you, he's the genuine article.'

She looked at him, her grey eyes huge with hurt and tiredness, and pushed her hair wearily away from her face. 'And Cam has got some things you'll never have . . . discernment, compassion and he loves people. He wouldn't take the word of a smart city lawyer.'

'Why did you lie to me, Serenity?' he asked quietly.

'Because you were such an easy mark,' she replied savagely and went back to the range scrubbing away her tears. She couldn't wait for Cam to come. He would comfort her. Even if she had done the things Hudson said, she knew Cam would have still tried to help her. Some things you knew without being told.

She served the meal, but the thought of eating was repugnant. 'Your dinner is served. I'll be in my room if Cam arrives.'

'I don't think I approve of your entertaining members of the opposite sex in your bedroom.' He attempted to say it lightly.

'That privilege reserved for the Boss only, is it?' Serenity said bitterly and started for the stairs.

'Serenity,' he called so sharply that she turned towards him. 'Come and join me at dinner. You've had a hard day. No breakfast, hardly any lunch, you must have some dinner.'

Her mouth quivered, 'No, thank you.'

Suddenly angry again, he sat down. 'If you want to starve yourself to death you'll get no sympathy from me.'

'I wouldn't expect any.' She continued up the stairs, then flung herself on her bed in a flood of tears. She had wanted to be alone to cry ever since Madeline had launched her attack. She had never been a cry-baby, but now she couldn't stop. But then she had never been so deeply hurt. Of course it was all her own stupid fault, that didn't help, it just made it so much worse.

Hudson had trusted her completely. Last night he had told Madeline that he would stake his reputation on her honesty. Last night he had kissed her. What a fool she had been. When she heard Cam drive up she went through to the bathroom and washed her face. There was no use trying to disguise the fact that she had been crying so she brushed her hair and put on some lipstick, then went downstairs.

Cam and Hudson were talking in the lounge, but as soon as Cam saw her he came straight to her.

'What's up, Serenity?'

'Don't give me sympathy, not yet. I'll cry over you,' she warned fiercely.

He put his arm about her and gave her a quick hug. 'I won't mind. Go ahead.'

She leaned against him for a moment, then she pushed him away. 'I'll clear up this mess, then I'll talk to you.'

Hudson stalked through. 'I'll leave you two on your own while I shoot over to see Tessa and Lee. Remember, Serenity, confession is good for the soul.'

Serenity winced and said to Cam, 'You can see how it is. And I've got to stay here.'

'I'll give you a hand to clear up here and you tell me all about it. Nothing is as bad as it seems.'

'This is.' Serenity told him everything, not sparing herself. When she had finished she demanded, 'Do you still believe me? Do you still think I told you the truth last night?'

'Of course I do. I'm sorry it came out this way but at least it's out in the open. Don't be too hard on Hudson, you're the first girl he's let get close to him for years and he feels you made a clown out of him. For a man with his sort of pride, that would be hard to take, especially in front of Madeline.'

'What will I do, Cam? I can't leave without seeming to be exactly what he called me. I can't stay with him hitting out at me all the time. Sure I get in a few licks of my own, but I don't enjoy trading cheap jibes. Not with someone I lo . . . liked so much.'

'Go on, say it. Someone you love.'

Serenity's voice was harsh. 'Someone I loved.' She gazed at him defiantly for a moment, then with a sob said in a low voice, 'Someone I love.'

'That's a brave girl, face your problem, then deal with it,' Cam encouraged her.

'How?' It was a wail.

'Come through to the lounge and we'll talk about it.' He sat on the sofa and patted the seat beside him.

Serenity slowly followed him and took her place. 'There's no way, Cam. He won't believe me. Even if I got John to come and tell him the truth he said he would know I had . . .'

'Yes, you told me all that. We'll forget that part. Remember this, he kept you here. Why do you think he did that?'

'To hurt me, to pay me back, he said as much.'

'Rubbish. I'll admit he's hurting and might want you

to suffer a bit too, but he wouldn't dare admit the real truth, that he didn't want to lose touch with you. You've made a breakthrough, that's the first time I've seen a chink in his armour-plating. Capitalise on it.'

'How?' This time there was a thread of hope in her voice.

'By loving him. By letting him see that you admire him, by caring for him the best way you know how, by never answering him back, no matter what he says to you.'

'I couldn't do that. He'd think he was right all the time, that I was trying to catch him. Anyway, when he's nasty, I just want to slam into him.'

Cam shrugged his shoulders. 'You asked me what to do. I don't mean you're to fawn over him and flatter him . . . nothing false. When he's rude keep your mouth shut, when he's pleasant answer him pleasantly.

'Now tell me how to do that,' she scoffed.

Cam grinned, 'By thinking of something nice and blotting out the hurt. You can think of me. Or think of Milo. Or think of the nicest thing Hudson did for you.'

'I'll never make it,' she protested.

'What's the alternative? Living here, snarling at each other every time you meet. Look, try it just for one day. Just one day at a time. Then come down each evening when I'm working Milo and blow your stack. I can take it.'

'I'll never make it,' she repeated slowly.

'Yes, you will, and the atmosphere will change, I promise you.'

'What have I got to lose? I'll give it a whirl.'

'What have you got to gain? Everything . . .'

They talked for a long time then Hudson joined them. 'Serenity been telling you the story of her life? I wonder which version you got, Cam? She's got a great imagination.'

Serenity felt Cam nudge her. She bit her lip to keep from shouting at him, then offered pleasantly, 'Would you like a cup of coffee, Hudson? Thanks for leaving us alone to have a talk. I feel much better.'

Hudson looked at her in surprise. 'Yes, I'd like coffee, how about you, Cam?'

'Thanks, Serenity, a good idea.'

She made some sandwiches, and put them with cakes and biscuits on a tray. As the men talked farming talk she steadily reduced the pile of sandwiches. An army marched on its stomach, and if it was going to be a battle, she intended going in well-equipped.

The food made her feel drowsy and she interrupted the men long enough to say goodnight and went to bed and fell asleep within seconds.

Next morning it wasn't such an effort getting out of bed. She had something to do. It was a Be-Nice-to-Hudson Day. What a challenge!

Serenity showered and dressed and went to the kitchen. She would be nice to him for one whole day even if it killed her, but only because Cam had asked her to do it.

'Good morning, Hudson,' she said cheerfully when he came in. 'Breakfast is ready.'

'Morning.' He sat down without a smile.

She sat down and started to eat her breakfast with every show of enjoyment, but his grimly held silence was a bit unnerving.

His breakfast finished, he stood up, 'You be ready and waiting at ten o'clock. We're heading for the Police Station, and bring some proof of identity.' He made it sound like a threat.

'Certainly.'

He glared, 'What are you so cheerful for? I'll be

standing right beside you to see that you don't tell any more lies.'

'I haven't told any lies,' she said carefully. 'Do you want another cup of tea?'

'No,' he snapped. 'You're up to something, I can tell, but don't think you're going to soft-soap me. If Cam has been feeding you some of his new-fangled psychology, forget it. It won't work.'

Her grey eyes sparkled. 'Oh, I don't think it's very new. Turn the other cheek and all that . . .'

'You turn the other cheek . . . very funny. You have to be on the other end of a dirty trick before you can do that, and you're the one who's been putting in the dirt, not me.'

'Hudson, please, I didn't mean to hurt you . . .'

'Hurt me, a little insignificant cheat like you . . . you've got to be joking. I'm only keeping you around to remind me what a fool I was to trust you, but you're a pretty expensive luxury. I have to waste a day trotting you into town, my men are going to waste a full day searching for your ring. I'm going to watch that you stay in your place, so I'll give the orders, you carry them out, and keep quiet while you get on with it.'

Serenity just looked at him, trying to think of Cam, of Milo, trying to blot out the pain of his words, but it didn't help.

His look was contemptuous. 'You've got nothing to say that's worth listening to, anyway. But while you're waiting for me, check out the stores and write a list. Tomorrow you'll have three extras for meals. Carpenters are coming to build a new barn.'

She watched him turn on his heel and make for his office. He knew very well she had no idea of ordering for a place this size. He was just hoping she would mess it up, then he would have further reason to sneer at her.

She did the housework, then dressed for town in a neat skirt and blouse. What did he mean, bring her credentials? She was the one who was robbed. She didn't have to prove anything.

As she started to check the pantry there was a knock on the door and a voice called, 'Anyone home?'

A stocky fair-haired man came in with a girl and two children. 'You'll be Serenity. Nice to meet you. I'm Lee, this is Tessa my wife, and our two youngest George and Gina. I've just popped up to talk business with Hudson—he said he'd be in the office. Tessa couldn't wait to make your acquaintance, so I'll leave you two to get talking.'

Tessa was slightly built with nut-brown hair and a sweet face. 'Hi, I hope I'm not in your road. Seeing as we're neighbours, I just thought I'd introduce myself and ask if you need any help.'

'Do I ever!' Serenity sighed thankfully. 'Hudson said for me to replenish the stores and I haven't a clue what to order or how much. Have you time to show me?'

'I heard you were friendly,' Tessa said happily, putting the wee girl down. 'You kids play outside. Now I'll check the basics and you write the list, then we'll brew up.'

The task was soon completed, and they were enjoying a cup of tea and laughing when Hudson came back with Lee.

'Will I get you two a cup of tea?' Serenity stood up quickly.

'I told you to be ready at ten. It is ten o'clock, get out to the car.'

Serenity turned, picked up her purse and the list, colouring slightly at the roughness of his tone to her in front of the others. She saw the surprise on their faces, and her smile was slightly wobbly. 'I'll see you two again,' she said as she walked out to the garage.

As Hudson joined her Lee called, 'Okay, Boss, I'll see to it,' and bitterly she decided she would never call him Hudson again. She'd call him Boss like the men did. The Be-Nice-to-Hudson Day was a pathetic idea.

Hudson never spoke all the way in to town, except for the one word 'list' when they stopped at the Creek. She watched him walk in and chat pleasantly with the Store people then saw his expression change back to hard grim lines as he got in beside her again.

He really hated her, and her heart ached at the loss of his friendship. It had really been so good, their short time together. And the misunderstanding *was* her fault. She would have to keep remembering that. He had really liked her, and was proving it by the bitterness he was showing. If he had not cared about her he wouldn't be so angry now. Suddenly the words he had used when he had been quarrelling with Madeline came back to her, 'I'd stake my reputation on her honesty.' It had warmed her then, but now it hurt unbearably. Cam was right, there was no point in them slashing at each other. If she could only hold her tongue, something still could happen to clear her, and they could part friends. If she gave back as good as she got the barrier between them would be so high, that when proven wrong, he would be even more angry.

She settled back comfortably in her seat. That was the nicest thing he had ever said, about staking his reputation on her honesty. When he hurt her she would remember that . . .

'Police Station, out you get.'

She stepped out on the footpath and nervously tucked in her blouse and brushed her hair away from her face.

'Trying for the wide-eyed innocent look again,' he sneered. 'You must have used it a lot to be so proficient.'

She didn't reply but quietly followed him into the
office, and noticed he greeted the sergeant by his Chris-
tian name. So he did know them well.

'So this is the young lady you told me about, Hudson.
You said you could vouch for her.'

As the sergeant pulled out a form Hudson said clearly,
'Oh, things have changed a bit since then, Mike. Miss
James is not the girl I thought she was, but she did arrive
wearing a ring and she says she lost it . . .'

'Well, that's the bit that concerns me. Now, Miss
James, tell me how it happened.'

When he had all the details, he said, 'Well, we have a
pretty wide field. Unless you are prepared to name
anyone specifically as a suspect, we really can't do a lot
of investigation. Can you give a name?'

'No.'

'Okay. Hudson said he'll take care of the wool bit, and
the men are searching the area today. That scanner is a
good idea. All we can do is put the details and number of
the ring on the Police Computer. If anyone has stolen it
and tries to sell it, or if it comes into our hands in the
future, we'll be able to identify it and get it back to you.'

'It's not hers,' Hudson said angrily. 'It belongs to the
Bellamy family. She wasn't supposed to have it in her
possession. So if you get it, don't let her get her hands on
it again. The engagement was broken off, she was
supposed to return it.'

The sergeant shot a questioning look at Serenity.

'It *was* mine. My fiancé rang me before he left the
airport and asked me to keep wearing it. He feels sure
we can work things out when he gets back, and he was so
upset that I agreed. John will verify this when he gets
back. But if you do trace it, I would rather you returned
it to him, not his family. It wasn't a family ring. He
bought it for me.'

'And you, Hudson, where did you get your information from?'

'From an impeccable source. John Bellamy's mother.'

'You spoke to her yourself?'

'No, but Miss Buchanan did. You've met her. She is unlikely to get her facts twisted.'

The sergeant looked from one angry face to the other then said simply, 'I prefer to leave this aspect until I talk to the young man himself. I have all the information I need just now. You'll let me know if you find it at Haupiri. Thank you both for coming in.'

Serenity said goodbye and went to the car with a jubilant spirit. He hadn't taken Hudson's word against hers, he hadn't believed Madeline or Mrs Bellamy, he wanted to hear from John. She was completely satisfied.

'You think you're so clever, don't you? Hudson said furiously as he flung himself into the seat.

'I don't, but I think the sergeant was. He's going to speak to John before he condemns me, but you couldn't wait that long.'

'You're still trying to claim you're innocent. You amaze me.'

Serenity sat still. There was no use talking to him. He had a closed mind.

He drove to the insurance company. 'Go in and see if your cheque is ready.'

When she came out she showed it to him. 'Thank you for bringing me in. I'll get a car and be back to work as soon as I can.'

'No, you don't. I'll go with you, then you can follow me home. That will make sure you do get there.'

She returned his gaze steadily. 'You shouldn't put such ideas in my head. You know I'm a weak character.' She got into the passenger seat and sat quietly.

He gave her a strange look. 'It's lunch time. We'll

have something to eat and you can tell me what make of car you want.'

She shrugged her slender shoulders, 'Whatever you say, Boss.'

Driving home behind him in her new car she felt more cheerful. She had seen his mouth tighten each time she called him Boss, and she knew he was sensitive enough to know why she was doing it. The drive out was lovely and the day hadn't been too bad. Tessa would be a real friend, and the police had accepted her story, and she really hadn't been rude to Hudson, so Cam would be pleased with her. When she saw the lake and the valley it felt like coming home, and her spirits soared. Maybe it would work out; just maybe Hudson would make his own enquiries after what the sergeant had said. Hudson was intelligent, when he wasn't angry. Hudson was wonderful. She started to sing 'Early one morning . . .'

The first week simply flew by, with Serenity being so busy she hardly had time to feel actively unhappy. With Hudson and the boys plus the carpenters to cook for she was fully occupied during the day and each evening she drove to the homestead and worked until midnight scanning the wool.

Hudson never missed a chance to whip her with his tongue, but as each day passed she became stronger in her resolve not to retaliate, and it became a battle of wills as he realised she was refusing to fight with him. It seemed to infuriate him, and his biting sarcasm became more cruel and taunting. Each night Cam joined her after he had worked with Milo and recounted how well the horse was progressing, and his praise for her restraint was sweet to her ears.

'Oh, Cam, if I didn't have you to encourage me, I'd pulverise him,' Serenity said as she rested on the edge of a bale of wool on the last night she was to spend on the wool. 'Today one of the boys asked about my family, and after they left, Hudson said he didn't believe my mother had died at all, that it was just another play for sympathy. He's so angry all the time and when the boys or the carpenters tease me or make me laugh he gets explosive. I don't think it would take a lot for him to really belt me.'

'He won't do that, Serenity, he's not the type. You're winning hands down, I tell you. He can't combat what you're doing, and he's probably hating himself for what he's doing. I was watching him the other day and he is tortured by doubts that he might be wrong about you. He said when I asked him that he had no complaints about your work, that you did everything cheerfully and willingly, and that the men thought the world of you. Of course he added that they were in for a shock when they found out what a phoney you were, but I could see he was truly puzzled. That crack about your mother was pretty tough, not like Hudson at all. Still, none of this behaviour is.'

'He's not the only one acting out of character. I could have killed him. This sweetness and light doesn't come naturally to me. I offered to go and get her death certificate and marriage licence for him and then realised I couldn't.'

'Why not? Didn't you have them with you?'

'Oh, I had them, but it would have given him information that I'm not prepared to share.' She had actually rushed to get them when she had seen Sarah Tarrant's name on the marriage licence and had had to come down and say to Hudson that, as he'd only say they were forgeries, she had decided against offering them.

Cam said with a sympathetic smile, 'I'll bet he made a mountain out of your not producing them. Let's get going and finish this lot.'

When the last bit of wool dropped into the bin, Serenity sagged. 'I knew it wasn't here. I hope he's not going to make me scan all these bales, the loose wool has been hard enough. He never even asked how I'm going, but he's been over to bale up when I'm not here, and it's gone for sure now. Thanks for helping me, but it's all been a waste of time. Oh, what a fool I was to lose it! I'm so tired, and we've done everything that's possible.'

'Not everything,' Cam said cheerfully. 'We'll pray about it. If we do the possible we can safely trust God to do the impossible.'

'You really believe that, don't you? My mother was just like you . . . Okay, I'm desperate enough to try anything. You go ahead.'

When Cam had said a simple prayer, he walked to the car with Serenity. 'What are you going to do tomorrow? It's Sunday. Will you come up home?'

'Thanks, but no thanks. I'm going to sleep all day.' Serenity stifled a yawn. 'I've never been so tired. Could I make it next weekend?'

'Sure thing. Don't go to sleep on the way home. And about the ring. It will turn up, but maybe not the way you expect.'

'Oh, Cam, I don't care how it's returned as long as I can give it back to John.'

The lights were still on when Serenity got home, and she wished she didn't have to face Hudson. Maybe he wouldn't speak to her.

'Did you find the ring?' he demanded as she walked in.

'No. And you knew I wouldn't. It was an exercise in futility, but at least it's finished.'

'Your part of it is. The trucks are coming Monday to take it to the auction in Christchurch, and the insurance company is going to meet it and try to find a scanner big enough to check the bales. Maybe the Airport will have

one, or the Hospital. I don't care what they do as long as
my wool doesn't miss the sale.'

'I'm sorry to have given you so much trouble . . .'

'I'm sure trouble is your second name. You're a real
jinx, aren't you? I've just had a call from Bill. Naomi is in
hospital in Greymouth and he's staying down there, so
I've got no one on the other side.'

'Well, you can't blame me for that, surely.'

'I have no doubt that as long as you stay here unfortunate happenings are going to be the order of the day.'
His hazel eyes were cold and unforgiving.

Serenity shrugged her shoulders. 'What do you want
me to do? Stay over the other side?'

His lips curved in a smile that held no humour. 'Only
for one day. You see, my father met up with a group of
farmers in Canada. They are coming out here on a tour
and he has offered them some fine West Coast hospitality. About six of them will be arriving to be entertained.
He suggests a barbecue, nothing but the best, Bar 2 beef
steaks, hogget chops, venison, mushroom, wine, silver
goblets—all the trimmings. Horse riding, sheep-dog
displays, with all the neighbours brought in to make
them feel welcome. As Naomi is out I'm nominating you
hostess, which I'm sure you'll carry out with your usual
flair.'

Serenity stared at him appalled. 'I haven't the foggiest
idea how to run something as big as that. You get your
tame lawyer over here, she'll do you proud.'

'I've given you the job. There'll be about a hundred
neighbours and friends that he'll want invited. I'll give
you a list, and when I'm certain of the date you can have
that, too. It will be the week after next probably. This
week we'll be doing the hay. Goodnight.'

Serenity sank into a chair. He was being ridiculous.
He was only trying to scare her. He was only waiting

until she made a huge mess of it and then he would sneer and call in Madeline. Oh Lord, help me out of this one, too. She grinned weakly. She must be catching something from Cam, asking for the impossible. But the thought of Cam cheered her. He would know how these things were done, and his parents would help her organise it. She climbed the stairs still smiling, her thoughts going to Madeline. If she wasn't invited to play hostess she would be livid, and Serenity felt that Hudson would be on the receiving end of a flow of invective that would make anything she had to say pale in comparison.

Another week passed and it was even more hectic than the first two. The carpenters were still putting the roof on the new barn as the first bales were being loaded in. Serenity managed to feed an ever-increasing army of men, answer a never silent phone, rush on frantic trips to the garage twenty miles away to get a tyre repaired for the tedder, then to get another part welded for the baler. But her great triumph of the week was a batch of scones she baked successfully under Tessa's careful tuition. And she had found time to make friends with Milo, now mouthed and ready for the saddle.

On Friday night all activity ceased, the hay was stored, the boys left for the weekend and she and Hudson were seated across the table for dinner, alone for the first time in a week.

'That was a fine meal, Serenity, thank you. And thanks also for a magnificent job this week.'

Serenity stared at him in amazement. A compliment! He must be sickening for something. Come to think of it, he had been acting a bit strangely all week, not friendly exactly, but dropping the aggressive rudeness, and treating her more or less like the rest of the staff. She had put it down to the fact that he had been too busy to concentrate on her.

'Well, the hay's in, so we can relax for a bit. We'll spend the weekend planning this barbecue, if that's okay with you.'

'I've accepted an invitation to stay with the Blairs,' Serenity replied and waited for a torrent of abuse.

'Yes, I suppose you're due for a bit of free time. I'll work on it myself then we'll go over it together when you get back.'

Stunned, Serenity watched him leave the room. A bubble of excitement welled up inside her and spread like a warm glow right through her whole being. He *had* changed. It wasn't just the excess of work. She tried to focus her mind on the past week, trying to pinpoint the last time he had let rip at her, and realised he hadn't been nasty since he had spoken about the barbecue. And he was going to plan it with her. They would be working *together* on the old footing. She felt as Cinderella must have done when the glass slipper had been fitted on her foot, weak with delight and feeling butterflies using her spine for a stepladder.

'Anybody home?'

Serenity froze. She would know those dulcet tones anywhere. Madeline was back.

'Oh, you're still here. Still sitting in the same old mess. Make me some coffee, please. Where's Hudson?'

'In his office. And I'm afraid you'll have to make your own coffee. I'm off duty for the weekend.' Serenity smiled wickedly. Cam had not said one word about not being nasty to Madeline.

The intelligent brown eyes glittered. 'How thoughtful of Hudson to get rid of you so that we can enjoy the weekend together.'

'I don't think he even knew you were coming,' Serenity replied smartly. 'I do hope it is a *pleasant* surprise.'

'Why, you little . . .'

'Insignificant cheat?' Serenity suggested, laughing. 'That's one of Hudson's. I'm sure you can do better.'

Madeline relaxed visibly. 'I won't descend to name-calling, but I am glad to hear Hudson is not letting you forget what you are. If he's making it all that unpleasant for you, why do you stay?'

Serenity said impudently, 'Because you forced me to. I had thought you would be more astute than that.'

Madeline glared. 'In what way?'

'Well, you put me on a spot. By dredging up that load of old rubbish with Mrs Bellamy, you undermined Hudson's opinion of me. I *had* to stay here and prove I was trustworthy, that I could complete a deal when I made it. I was planning to leave the very afternoon you floored me with your great denouncement.'

'And have you proved your, excuse me for laughing, trustworthiness?' The brown eyes shone dangerously.

'I'm working on it,' Serenity informed her cheerfully. 'You know, in olden times, the saints used to whip themselves, and mortify themselves by walking miles with hard peas in their shoes to humble themselves and show God they loved him. I haven't quite taken it to that length, but I've been close.'

Madeline pounced, 'So you do love Hudson. I was right.'

'Yes, you were right, Madeline. So if you'd been really as clever as you're credited to be, you would have been working to prove that I was telling the truth. That way Hudson would have been so sorry that he "had done me wrong" that he'd have called the deal off, and, honour satisfied, I could have left the field clear for you.'

'A likely story. If you had been proved in the right, you'd have stuck like glue and tried to manipulate him to the altar. Your sort never give up . . .'

'And neither do yours,' Serenity cried scornfully. 'But

as for me dragging a reluctant Hudson to face the preacher man, he's the last person I'd marry.'

'Why do you say that? Not that I believe you, of course.'

'It is a matter of small concern to me whether you believe me or not. You seem to have remarkable difficulty in discerning the truth. I hope you never make it to the judge's bench, or justice in this country would suffer a severe set-back. However, seeing as you're part of Hudson's future, I feel it's only fair to tell you I have no intention of upsetting your plans. I didn't come here to cause trouble.'

'You haven't answered me. Why wouldn't you marry Hudson? Not that you'd ever get the chance, but I am curious.'

'Because when I marry a man, I'm going to love him forever, and I would expect to be loved, cherished and protected by him. Hudson doesn't want anything as sentimental as love in his marriage, so you'll suit him fine. Another thing he told me in the first few days was that no woman would ever be indispensable in his life. Well, I'm going to be indispensable to my husband, I'm going to come first in his life, I'm going to make him so comfortable, so happy, that when I'm not with him, life won't even feel real to him. I'm not like you, I have no intention of settling for second-best. He's only half a man. I don't want a man who is incapable of love. I've got a lot to offer some man, but not Hudson Grey. Lady, he's all yours.'

Hudson's voice from the foot of the stairs made them both jump. 'I'd like to see you in the office before you leave, Serenity. Hullo, Madeline, come through to the lounge and have a drink before you unpack.'

Serenity was hardly aware of the two of them moving away, and even though she could hear the murmuring of their voices in the next room she tried to concentrate on clearing the table. She must have been out of her mind to speak out so baldly to Madeline, not that she would take one word back. She had just not wanted Hudson and Madeline spoiling their weekend squabbling about her. She wouldn't have minded spoiling Madeline's weekend but Hudson didn't need any more strife.

She went upstairs and collected her bag. Praise the Lord for the Blairs' invitation. Imagine if she had been locked up here with those two for forty-eight hours. She tapped on the office door. Strange how calm she felt, even knowing that she had admitted loving Hudson and that there was a distinct possibility that he had overheard her. Well, if he had heard that he would have also heard that as husband material she rated him less than adequate.

'Come along in, Serenity.'

Her chin lifted defiantly as she heard the old touch of amusement in his voice. 'I hope you'll keep it short, I want to get up the valley before dark.'

'Oh, Serenity, welcome back. To hear you chew Madeline out was a real tonic. I thought you'd forgotten how to keep your end of an argument up. You were really sparking on all cylinders. I thought that meek mild turn-the-other-cheek was going to be permanent. A terrifying thought.'

'Cam didn't say I wasn't to be rude to Madeline,' she said aggressively, her eyes sparkling.

'He probably never thought of it. But why did he protect me from the viper tongue?'

Serenity shrugged her shoulders, there seemed no point in not telling him. 'Because, he said, if I slashed you back each time you hurt me, and one day you found out I was telling the truth, you'd be even more angry than at first.'

'A wise friend you have in Cam, that's obvious. Because I believe you were telling the truth and that we misunderstood each other. And because you have patiently borne the slings and arrows of outrageous fortune that I've seen fit to hurl at you, I am now deeply humiliated by my behaviour. Will you forgive me, Serenity? I know no apology can cover the treatment I've dished out to you, but somehow I'm confident that you're big enough to forgive and forget.'

Serenity sighed with relief. 'It's a pleasure, Boss. It's wiped out, gone and forgotten. How did you find out? Did you catch up on John?'

'No Serenity, I caught up with my own common sense. I should have trusted my own judgment from the first.'

'Ooh! You mean you've got no proof.' Her grey eyes widened.

'Not one iota. I don't need it. But I can't accept your forgiveness is fact until you go back to calling me Hudson. That irritating habit of calling me Boss with every second breath has driven me insane.'

Serenity giggled happily, 'I thought it might, Hudson.' It was so wonderful to be friends with him again, so wonderful to have him trust her, so wonderful to be able to laugh with him, so wonderful . . . so wonderful.

'And until you meet up with Cam, you're still pledged to be nice to me. Is that correct?' He stood up from his desk and walked towards her, smiling.

'Not nice, just not rude,' Serenity answered a little breathlessly, edging towards the door.

'That'll do fine. I always feel a kiss shows true forgiveness. When I was small my mother always used to make me kiss and make up, and until now I never saw the full value of her teaching.'

'No, Hudson. No!' She tried in vain to hold him off but

knew joyfully that she would fail. She responded to the touch of his mouth on hers with a passion that equalled his, and then rested in his arms content and secure and spent.

'Will you marry me, Serenity?'

She stiffened and pulled away from him. 'I will not! I would never marry you. You heard me tell Madeline. How dare you ask me?'

'How dare you refuse me, darling? I heard you state clearly that you love me, and you've assured me you always tell the truth.'

'I do. And I'm leaving, now that we've got that misunderstanding settled.'

He pulled her back into his arms, and held her easily, smiling down at her flushed, protesting face, his hand tenderly brushing her fair hair back, and tracing the contours of her cheek and throat. 'I think I'm finding that I've made one mistake after another. I've a horrible feeling that you are indispensable to my happiness. I think I could love you, Paleface.'

Serenity gulped, and in a husky voice retorted, 'Don't force yourself, because I won't marry you. I know your ideas on marriage. They aren't mine, neither are your moral standards. I'm not criticising, I'm just saying we're different. I can't stay here with you, now you know how I feel about you.'

'A deal is a deal. You're here for another two weeks.'

'That's not fair.'

'You've had a chance to prove your word, Serenity. Aren't you going to give me a chance to prove mine? When I make a deal, when I make a commitment, it stands. I will have the same attitude to marriage.'

'Go and tell Madeline, she'll be delighted.' Serenity ducked under his arm and grabbed her bag and stood outside the door breathing jerkily. 'I thought you didn't

need to poach on another man's territory. I'm engaged
to John until I get that ring back.'

'And when you get the ring back, and return it, then
you'll be a free agent?'

'I suppose so,' Serenity said shakily.

'Good, then that's settled. You stay on here, and I'll
treat you with the utmost circumspection and propriety,
unless you ask me to do otherwise.'

'Ever the optimist.' Serenity was getting her courage
back now that she wasn't so close to him. 'I'll talk to
Cam . . .'

Anger flared suddenly in his hazel eyes. 'Cam isn't
God, you know.'

'No, but he's a good representative. Have a nice
weekend.' She ran lightly down the stairs and out to her
car.

CHAPTER EIGHT

She was trembling so much she could hardly get the key in the switch, and she felt on the edge of panic until she turned for the main road. She was well out of her depth. Her heart was pounding as if she had run a four-minute mile. Hudson had asked her to marry him. In spite of her scathing remarks to Madeline, about Hudson being only half a man, she knew that half of Hudson, the half he was prepared to give, was more than the complete whole of any two other men.

She loved Hudson Grey with every fibre of her being. How could she live in that house with him for another two weeks? She knew now that he wanted her, but it was only a physical want, a temporary thing, while her need was for a permanent and enduring relationship. Not that hers wasn't a physical desire also. She still felt the pressure of his lips on hers, the warmth and comfort of his body against hers, and the barely controlled passionate longing to demand more and more from him, to give herself without restraint, to be wholly and totally satisfied, united and part of that tremendous strength and vitality that flowed from him.

It was a primitive urge, of such burning intensity that it scorched her like a flame when he held her in his arms, beyond any experience or understanding she possessed. No wonder she had felt danger all around her in Sarah Tarrant's garden, and in the office tonight; not danger from him but from herself, and her instinct was to run, to put distance between them was sheer self-preservation. Something had been kindled between them that very first morning when he had carried her up to his Land-Rover, and she had snuggled into his arms, enjoying a sensation strange and wonderful beyond description, an exhilaration and bubbling happiness that had made her laugh and sing with him.

She parked on the bluff, looking over the glorious valley, trying to find that quality of peace that was so much part of the beauty of it, the lush green pastures stretching for miles, sloping down to the lake, ringed by the hills and mountains, secret and secluded and still. Unconsciously her eyes found Hudson's house just below Brian O'Lynn, and she knew her instinct to run was fading, and the longer she stayed near him, the harder it would be to leave.

Impatiently she eased the car back on to the road and swept down the steep hill to cross the swift flowing Haupiri river and headed for the Blairs'. Hudson had offered to marry her, but so casually, as if one girl was no different from another. She wanted more than that, but Cam would advise her. Cam might tell her to leave, she cringed away from the thought. Her love for Hudson was blotting out natural caution, like the moon eclipsing the sun. The earth about her darkened at the thought of not being with him.

She enjoyed the weekend but Hudson was never out of her thoughts. Time away from him lacked zest, no matter how nice people were, they seemed dull compared to the vibrant vitality of his personality, and the sheer fascination of being in his presence. His offer of marriage had brought nothing but confusion. She wanted time, time for him to get to know her, for herself to know him, yet she knew he wouldn't give her that time.

As she drove up the narrow road towards Hudson, she tried to suppress the simmering sense of expectancy bubbling within her. And she would be able to tell him she was Sarah Tarrant's granddaughter.

Robert Blair had taken her aside and given her a cutting from an old newspaper. 'This notice was in all the papers, Serenity, for months after Sarah Tarrant died. The lawyers were trying to trace her daughter. I can only presume that your mother never saw it. I have wondered why you have not claimed the relationship, you are perfectly entitled to do that. I can assure you that no one will be hurt by such a disclosure, there was no public scandal. The estate is not inconsiderable and I advise you to get in touch with these people immediately.'

Serenity had been grateful that he had offered the information in such a matter-of-fact way, but what would Hudson think? Would he think that she had been devious in not telling him straight away? She couldn't bear another misunderstanding. The money wasn't important, although it would be nice to be financially secure—she would rather be secure in Hudson's love, but there was no guarantee of that. But she was kin to Sarah Tarrant and the thought delighted her. If she married Hudson it would be like a dowry, a blessing from Sarah for their happiness.

She slammed on the brakes in front of the house, furious with the direction her thoughts had carried her. She was scared that Hudson would rush her into a decision and here she was out-distancing him by a mile. Flushed she picked up her case and headed for the house, hoping she would find him absent. She needed time.

'Had a good weekend?' Hudson greeted her with an endearing grin.

'Lovely, thank you.' Serenity answered, a little over effusively, glancing around the lounge to see if Madeline was still about.

'Madeline has gone. She won't be back.'

'Oh, why?' She took a seat as far away from him as possible.

'I told her I was going to marry you. She didn't take it very well.' His hazel eyes sparkled wickedly, waiting for her reaction.

'She had good reason to be angry. You've been playing fast and loose with her. I don't know why she bothered with you. I won't. It's a pity she didn't check with me, as I would have told her that I have no intention of accepting your elegantly worded proposal.'

'Oh, you want an old-fashioned-style proposal, me down on my knees. For you, Serenity, I'll even go that far.' In one lithe movement he was out of his chair and moving towards her.

She jumped up and met him half-way. 'Don't make yourself ridiculous. I have no intention of marrying you . . .'

'And I have every intention of marrying you.' He swooped her up in his arms and carried her back to a low lounge chair, easily holding her a prisoner while he dropped to his knees. 'Serenity James, will you do me the immense honour of accepting my hand in marriage . . . ?'

'Never,' Serenity struggled furiously to dislodge his arm.

'I haven't finished,' Hudson said calmly. 'You will become bone of my bones, flesh of my flesh, and cleave only unto me, and you'll comfort and cherish me, so that when we are apart I'll find the world unreal.'

She became still, her eyes dark and enormous, her face only inches away from his. 'I can't.'

'Why not?' he demanded.

'Because you treat marriage as a joke. Until this morning you were going to marry Madeline. You don't love me. You are just momentarily attracted to me. Next week it might be someone else.'

'Last month you were going to marry John,' he pointed out quickly. 'This morning you told Madeline that you loved me. What's the difference?'

She was wavering, she longed to say yes, to put her arms about him to draw him to her, and sensing her indecision he leaned forward and kissed her gently.

When he lifted his head he saw the tears sliding down her cheeks, and releasing her, lifted her on to his knee, cradling her tenderly. 'Why are you fighting me, Serenity? I accept that you love me, accept it with great happiness. But you refuse to believe me when I tell you with all sincerity that I love you and want to marry you. What are you scared of?'

Serenity scrubbed her eyes, 'You haven't got a great track record. I can't help hearing things living here. You stopped loving and trusting people when your girl died. You've just used women since then.'

'Yes, I admit that, but I feel differently about you. Don't you credit me with the ability to change if I really want to?'

'I just don't believe you love me enough to change so drastically. You're used to changing partners when you're bored. You'd tire of me.'

'What do I have to do to prove that I love you and that I'll be faithful.'

'I don't know,' she said honestly.

'So you're setting me an impossible task. Keep on talking and maybe we'll come up with a solution. What else troubles you?' His lips brushed lightly over her hair down her cheek and then to her mouth.

Cam had said she was strong, but she wasn't, she was weak and crumbling. She loved his caresses, and she loved his kisses, and she seemed to be fighting herself as much as him.

'Your attitude to marriage is lighthearted, the throwaway mentality. I'm not like that. And stop kissing me, I can't think straight. That's another thing, you think I'm funny because I don't hop in and out of bed with anyone I fancy.'

'I don't think you're funny, I think you're entrancing. I admire your thinking and that you have waited for me.'

Serenity sat up angrily. 'I didn't wait for you. I've waited for the man I'm going to marry. You don't even understand my thinking much less admire it.'

'Don't get so ruffled. I'm just an old cynic and I shouldn't tease you, but I find it irresistible. If you would explain how you came to this decision I'm sure I would approve.'

Serenity stood up. 'You're just kidding me along. But it *is* important to me. I don't want to enter marriage with hangups of guilt and regrets. It's a matter of knowing your self worth. I know who I am, I don't have to sleep around to have people tell me I'm loved or I'm desirable.'

'I'm so sure you're right.' His mouth quirked but he resisted the temptation to smile. 'And you despise everyone who enjoys sex outside of marriage.'

'*No. I do not*,' Serenity glared at him. 'I knew you wouldn't understand. It's a personal decision. I've got lots of friends who sleep around and that life-style suits them fine, it doesn't make them better than me, or worse than me. I work with girls who have lived with their men for a couple of years and then married them, and in some cases it's worked out wonderfully well, but it would be wrong for me. I know that. I've seen girls who have gone against their own better judgment and slept with a guy because they loved him and I've seen the scars they wear when it's over. It's too big a risk.'

'And where did you get this very tender conscience from?' Hudson asked.

'From my mother,' Serenity replied truthfully. 'She messed up her own life, her own marriage, and almost destroyed a very good man. She talked to me a lot; she didn't want me to make the same mess that she did. She said sex was a great and wonderful natural force, like electricity: out of control like lightning it can burn down a building in a blazing holocaust, destroy in minutes what it has taken years to build, but harnessed like electric power it can bring heat and light into your life through the years and provide blessings to all who love you.'

Somehow she was back in his arms, not even knowing she had moved.

'Serenity, tell me, have you had a great deal of trouble avoiding the holocaust?' He was smiling down at her.

'No. None at all, not till now, not until I met you.' She saw the light flare in his eyes, and his lips came down on hers and she gave herself to the sweetness of the moment, knowing as the fire in her rose to meet his demand that she had no strength left to deny him whatever he asked. When the raging inferno seemed to reach its peak, Hudson suddenly held her away from him. 'You'll stay here for two more weeks, Serenity?'

'Yes, I will.' She had no strength left to refuse.

The strident ring of the telephone came like a miracle.

'Saved by the bell,' Hudson said with a grin. 'I'll answer it, because I don't want to be disturbed for a while. I'll take if off the hook. Now don't you go sloping off to bed, because you and I have things to talk about. If you go to bed, I'll join you, so give it considerable thought.' He gave her an eloquent look as he strode for his office.

With burning cheeks, Serenity moved swiftly on to the patio, loving the coolness of the night air on her face. She wanted to run, to flung her case in her car and drive and drive, yet as Hudson had said that night in Sarah's garden . . . it was too late. So this was the fire that her mother had warned her of, this ecstasy of love, this exhilaration of the senses, this anguish and this joy. An inferno which, once ignited, could flare into a consuming conflagration which could, uncontrolled, destroy in minutes one's cherished ideals.

She gazed at the beauty of the night, the loveliness of the stars and mountains, and was deeply grateful that she had this breathing space to sort out her thoughts. She had no doubt now of the power of the attraction between them, or of her weakness in the face of Hudson's demands, but if he pressured her into a decision against her principles she would live to regret it. Her conviction was an essential part of her personality, maybe even the very part of her that drew him to her.

'Are you there, Serenity?'

Trembling, she brushed her hair back from her face and walked back into the lounge.

'I'm glad I answered that phone call. You'll never guess who was calling. John Bellamy! I told him you weren't available, but if he liked to ring back later you'd be happy to talk to him.'

Anger lit her grey eyes. 'What right had you to make that decision? I *need* to talk to John.'

'We have some things to settle first. He's not at all upset about the ring, only distressed that his mother might have given people down here the wrong impression. He sounds a pleasant chap.'

'He's a wonderful man, and I'm furious at your arrogant action in saying I wasn't available. That was a lie.'

'You aren't available to anyone until we've finished talking. I am happy to say he has released you from the engagement. I told him I had asked you to marry me, and that you loved me. He was very generous, and offered me his congratulations. He said you deserved the best, and he was sorry that he'd mucked up his chances.'

'How could you? I could . . .' Serenity spluttered in anger, too upset to find the words she needed. 'You deliberately said it that way so that he would miscontrue the whole situation. When he rings back, I'll set him straight. I . . .'

'I told no lies,' Hudson said calmly. 'I was as honest with him as you were with me when you arrived. Isn't that true?'

Serenity swallowed with difficulty, wanting to scream at him, but knowing it was no different. She had told the truth, but not the whole truth. Hudson had done the very same thing. How could he have been so cruel to John? John had come back hoping to fix things up, and Hudson had baldly told him she was already in love with another man. She could kill him. She fought back the torrent of rage that threatened.

'You had no right, Hudson Grey,' was all she could manage, in a shaking voice. 'No right at all.'

'I had every right, Serenity. I have cleared away my past. I have sent Madeline away. We could not talk honestly until John had given you his clearance. Well, we have that. Now we can talk.'

'I have nothing to say to you. You're . . . you're a monster.'

Hudson threw back his head and roared laughing. 'Not exactly a warm declaration of love. But you do love me, Serenity. Deny it if you can.'

Serenity bit her lip. Was it possible to love someone and hate them at the same time? Because that was exactly how she felt, all mixed up.

'What would you have said to John? Can you tell him you want to marry him?'

'No, I can't, but I would have . . .'

'Broken it to him gently,' Hudson threw at her scornfully. 'Would you have jollied him along for a few months, trying to soften the blow? There is no way to give that news gently. It probably hurt him like hell, but it had to be done. You should be grateful that I told him.'

'Well, I'm not,' Serenity replied fiercely. 'You had no right.'

'You're repeating yourself, my darling. I have the right to pursue my own happiness, and it's all wrapped up in you. I'm going to marry you.'

'I'll never marry you. You're cruel and insensitive, and . . .'

'I love you, and you love me.' He caught her in his arms, and kissed her until she stopped fighting him.

'Talk about the taming of the shrew,' he said, laughing down at her.

Serenity wrenched herself away from him. 'I'm not a shrew. And you're very experienced at making love, but that doesn't prove anything. Love is more than a physical response.'

'I know, but it helps to know that you're so *responsive*,' he said with a wicked grin. 'Now we'll have a cup of coffee, and discuss this sensibly.'

Serenity marched off to the kitchen indignantly, and plugged in the kettle. Of course he was right, John had to be told, and now it was done she felt a huge sense of relief. But need she be such a push-over every time Hudson kissed her? And she wouldn't marry him. Who would want to be tied to a man who took everything into his own hands? Not her.

'Put the supper on the table, Serenity. You sit on one side, me on the other, and we'll talk. With this broad expanse of solid *kauri* between us, you won't be able to accuse me of trying to confuse you with an emotional appeal.'

Serenity sat opposite him, knowing that if they put the Pacific Ocean between them, the very thought of him would still stir her senses beyond ordinary caution.

He was silent for a considerable time, then looked at her, all laughter gone from his eyes, so serious that it scared her.

'You don't want me to make love to you, you don't want to marry me, so there's nothing left for me to do but tell you to pack your bags and leave. Is that what you really want, Serenity?'

The pain of his words, the unexpectedness of them, was like a violent physical blow. He was telling her to go, he was sending her away . . . She closed her eyes, letting her long lashes rest on her pale cheeks so that he could not read the despair she felt. 'I'll leave tonight,' she said in a low voice.

'What other option have I? What do you really want?'

'I would like time, time for us to get to know each other,' she said, trying to stop herself from crying. He wasn't going to give her that . . .

'Time would not change how I feel about you, Pale-face, and I don't think you'd know me any better than you do this minute, even if you stayed here a year. You wanted an old-fashioned proposal; do you want an old-fashioned courtship, too? How long would it take you to learn to trust me? A year? Two years? You couldn't stay here alone with me. I'm not made of iron. Do you think if I spent hours whispering sweet nothings in your ears, or if I sent you flowers and gifts for a year, you'd know me one whit better than you do now? You've got to take me on trust, as I do you.'

'You don't know me at all,' Serenity said stubbornly.

'I know all I want to know about you. Go on, surprise me. Tell me something about yourself that would shock me, change my attitude towards you.'

'I'm Sarah Tarrant's granddaughter,' she flung at him angrily.

His eyes softened remarkably. 'Of course, I should have known.' His strong tanned hand stretched across the table and enveloped here. 'No wonder you're so strange and wonderfully different from any other girl I've ever met. She was superb, my friend Sarah. And it was in her garden I first kissed you, and first knew I loved you. How she must have chuckled.'

'Don't you think I'm devious and underhanded, sneaking my way in here, not being completely honest for coming?' She was trying to needle him, trying to hurt him, and not even understanding herself.

'Not at all. You said it was confidential; I presume you had your reasons. You'll tell me in your own good time. You know, after I lost Emma, Sarah was the only one I could talk to, and she told me that some day I'd meet a girl who would be a match for me in every way. And she said that when I did, the love that I had lost would be but a pale shadow of that which I found. That's true, Serenity; she was talking about her own granddaughter.'

There was such a wealth of tenderness and love in his expression that Serenity found all her objections sliding away. She loved him, she wanted to be with him always, and she admired and respected him. Now she knew he loved her, that she could trust him to the uttermost. She didn't know how she had come by that knowledge, it had just happened.

'What do you want, Hudson?' she asked at last.

'Ah, now you're talking. I want to marry you, now, Serenity. I asked you once whether John was man enough for the road you wanted to walk. He wasn't, but I am. There's no road, however rough, that you will take that I won't match you step for step, and pick you up and carry you if you falter. I will cherish you, love you, protect you, but I am and always will be head of the house. I will respect your wishes, when you show common sense . . .'

'I always do that,' Serenity interrupted quickly.

'Not always, mostly. This waiting game isn't for me, nor for you. We'd only be wasting precious time. We've got years to spend together, getting to know each other. Now you name the day when you will marry me.'

Serenity withdrew her hand from his clasp, and immediately felt cold and shivery. The warmth and glowing happiness that had filled her as he declared his love fell away, and her mouth went dry. Fear clawed at her, deep down within, as she realised she must answer him. He was offering her all she had ever dreamed of, and more, yet she was frightened to reach out and take such happiness.

'What is it, Serenity? What is the matter?' he demanded sharply, aware of the change in her attitude.

She shook her head. 'I'm sorry, I can't.'

'But you have to. You can say yes, and it's all over bar the shouting and celebrations, or you can say no, and I will not ask you again. I have found this weekend very exhausting; I am not prepared to go through it again. I have to have a definite answer tonight. Take your time, think about it, then answer me. You can say next week, next month or next year. I will abide by what you say.'

She bit her lip. Where had this panic come from? Why? She loved him, she trusted him, and yet . . . Then she realised that the fault was in herself, not in him. She had thought that she had come through the collapse of her marriage plans without much hurt, but it wasn't true. She was scared of a repeat performance, and this time it would be much worse, because this time she was really in love. She wouldn't survive rejection a second time round.

He sat there patiently, not hurrying her, but he was waiting for an answer, determined to have one. She hadn't met his parents. What if they reacted to her the way Madeline had, the way Mrs Bellamy had, making her feel insignificant and worthless? She hadn't cared very much about Mrs Bellamy's opinion of her. She was a joke to most people in the town, in spite of her position; they had laughed at her arrogance, her superior airs, and her mania for head-hunting prominent people for trophies at her parties. She had been a social climber of the worst variety, and her snide innuendoes had slidden off Serenity as water off a duck's back, because she considered her blatant and slightly vulgar.

But Hudson's parents were different. She would need their good opinion, she would want it, if the marriage were to be a success. She had no way of knowing what their reaction would be. She knew that there was nothing false or artificial about them. The visitors who had come through since she'd been there had shown, by their genuine disappointment, how loved and respected they were. She had seen Hudson's photo album, photos of his parents taken with the Prime Minister, photos of Hudson with the Governor General's sons when they had been visiting the Bar 2. How could she expect them to accept a girl like her, without a background?

If she accepted Hudson, said she would marry him next month, and they came home and were disappointed in her, she wouldn't marry him. How could she answer him? Mrs Bellamy's words came pounding into her brain: 'a nice enough girl, a bit nondescript, no background, no breeding . . .' Desperately she wanted her mother, someone to advise her. Dear God, she prayed silently, closing her eyes tightly, give me wisdom.

'Well, Serenity, I think you've had long enough,' Hudson said firmly.

Serenity opened her eyes. 'I'll give you an answer when the ring is found. You said yourself that I wouldn't be a free agent until I had handed it back.'

With uncanny perception he said, 'You're looking for a sign; that will be okay. I accept that, because I believe that we are right for each other. I'd like you to be sure, too. I don't think it was coincidence that you came to Haupiri at this particular time. Now, how long after the ring is found until our wedding day?'

'When the ring is found, I'll marry you any day *you* choose.'

'Great, let's drink to that.' He walked through to the lounge and came back with glasses and wine. 'I'm glad that's settled.'

'But you don't know if it will be found?' Serenity protested with flushed cheeks.

'It will be found,' he answered confidently, touching his glass to hers. 'To our future, Serenity.'

'You're impossible,' she exclaimed, but she drank the toast.

He laughed jubilantly. 'Exactly what my mother calls my father, a good omen, because they've always been very happy. Talking of my parents, they'll want to be here for the wedding, so I'll ring them tonight. My father will want to make the arrangements and he has a special flair for organising splendid occasions, so be assured that your wedding will be like no other.' He bent his head and kissed her. 'Now that is the last kiss I will give you until the ring is found. Who would you like to have as guests for the wedding?'

'You're going too fast,' Serenity spluttered. 'Find the ring first.'

He pulled a notebook from his pocket. 'Names and addresses, please, phone numbers if you have them, because when this ring is found they will have to be flown in. I will brook no delays.'

Somehow Serenity found herself giving Barbie's and Robbie's names, then Dr Saveny and his wife, and the Matron, and several others.

'Now off to bed, Paleface, I've got a lot of work to do and hours on the telephone.'

She left him writing in his notebook. Didn't he want to kiss her goodnight? Apparently not. At the door she turned. 'Thank you for making it so easy, Hudson.'

'Speak for yourself, it's not easy for me.' But his smile had all the old charm. Then he started writing again.

She went to bed, her mind in a turmoil, excited and scared in equal parts. Cam had prayed that the ring would be returned, so that if it came back her marriage would be blessed, if it didn't . . . no, she wouldn't think about that. It was out of her hands now.

Hudson didn't kiss her the next morning either—and she wanted to be kissed. He had said not till the ring was found, so when was it going to be found?

'My parents are flying home, they'll be here at the weekend,' he informed her as she put his breakfast in front of him. 'We've got a lot to get through this week. We start the muster this morning; the calves must be marked and weaned over the next few days. A bullock must be chosen for the barbecue, and the wood got ready. My father was very specific in his instructions, only *matai*, that is black pine, to be used for cooking the steaks; the coals retain the heat and give the meat a

subtle flavour. And he wants the famous Kokatah
Band—they played for the Queen when she came to the
West Coast. He wants nothing but the best for the
wedding.'

'They're pleased with the news?' she asked nervously.
'Delighted.'

'You told them about the ring? No ring, no wedding.'

'Yes, I told them. Now we've got a big day on cattle
work, let's get at it.'

They didn't only have one big day; they had four big
days working with the cattle, mustering the riverbed,
drafting and marking and weaning the calves, and she
hardly saw Hudson alone all week, and he never kissed
her, not *once*. He seemed preoccupied, obsessed with
the work, remote from her, and spent every spare
minute on the phone.

On Friday night he announced he was off to Christchurch for the weekend and dressed in his city best he
seemed a suave and sophisticated stranger.

She stood by his car to say goodbye, hoping he would
say why he was going, or that he would miss her. If he
was meeting his parents, why didn't he take her?

'Cam's spending the day with you tomorrow. Your
first day on Milo. Be careful and have a good time.'

He drove off leaving her forlorn and depressed, and
unkissed. Apart from his conversation at breakfast on
Monday he had not mentioned the wedding, nor even
that he was doing anything extra to find the ring. Was he
just waiting for someone to drop it into his lap? Or
maybe he didn't care any more. Was he bored already?
Was he driving to spend the weekend with Madeline?
Some previous engagement he had with her?

She walked slowly down to Sarah Tarrant's house,
ignoring Bambi's attempts to play with her. She was too
miserable. She had promised Tessa to babysit the chil-

lren and it was nice to feel she could repay a little of the
kindness Tessa had given her. Oh, was she just a *gullible*
fool? Was Hudson the hunting type of male and the
conquest less important than the chase? She had been
such a push-over.

She loved her time at the old house but when Tessa
and Lee came home she refused to stay the night, and
hurried back to fling herself on her bed in floods of tears.
How could she ever have expected to hold the love of a
man like Hudson Grey? He was an experienced man of
the world. Had he been just amusing himself with her? If
so, she had been a *pathetic* lump, being so honest with
him, sharing thoughts she had never expressed to anyone before. Had he been laughing all the time, amused
by her naive ideas on love and sex and marriage?

Saturday was spent with Cam. Serenity had so looked
forward to her first long ride on Milo, picturing herself
riding with Hudson, but now she was glad that he was
miles away on the other side of the mountains. Milo was
a fantastic horse, full of fire and spirit and she was glad,
too, that she had to concentrate her whole attention on
him, as she galloped beside Cam towards Fisher's Gorge
where they were to have their picnic.

'Glad to see the colour back in your face, Serenity.
You looked a bit woebegone when I arrived. Missing
Hudson?'

'No, I'm not,' Serenity said staunchly gathering her
pride about her.

'Along here's the hot springs,' Cam announced as he
swung down from his saddle. 'You can enjoy sitting with
one foot in hot water and the other in the ice-cold
Haupiri. There was a time when they discussed turning it
into a tourist attraction, but I'm glad it didn't come off.
Imagine this place filled with hoards of litterbugs.'

'Awful,' Serenity agreed, looking at the steep-sided

mountain gorge and the towering Mt Elizabeth soaring above them.

'Are things well between you and Hudson? Sorry haven't been able to catch up on you this week.'

Serenity hesitated, then it all came spilling out, about the marriage proposal, about being Sarah's granddaughter. 'I said I'd marry him if the ring was found Cam. Was that an awful thing to say, like tossing a coin?'

'Not at all like tossing a coin, you're just handing the decision over to a higher authority.' His bright blue eyes smiled warmly at her.

'But what about his parents?' she cried anxiously. 'I'm terrified. What if they are like the Bellamys?'

'They are not in the least like the Bellamys. They will accept you for what you are, a darling girl. They will respect Hudson's judgment, and his choice of wife Make him happy and you'll make them happy.'

'You make it all sound so easy,' she said doubtfully wanting reassurance.

'It is easy,' he told her. 'Remember you're Sarah Tarrant's granddaughter. She was highly respected in this district. Don't be scared of his father, he's got an excellent sense of humour and a splendid sense of the ridiculous. You'll like him, that's a promise. Anyone who meets him is richer for that experience, and better yet, no one is ever the poorer for it. Does that make you feel better?'

'You always make me feel better,' Serenity smiled. 'You know I used to be so sure of myself and confident but since I've arrived at the Haupiri, I've been so silly not knowing whether to go or whether to stay, and then hesitating about accepting Hudson when I need him so much. I hope I'm not going to become permanently dithery.'

Cam laughed, 'You're not the type. You've been

hrough a tough time, that's all. Go and change and soak
ll your cares away in the hot springs.'

Next morning she wandered about the house restless
nd unsettled. It was so lonely without Hudson, unbear-
ble. She caught Milo and saddled up. She would ride
lown the Seven Hundred and look at the huge project
Hudson and his father had undertaken to bring hun-
lreds of acres of swamp land into healthy pastureland.
She'd read about it in a farming magazine and they had
lescribed it as real 'tiger country', and she wanted to see
now they had tamed and cultivated it.

Hours later, heading for home, she saw Lee galloping
owards her. Reining in beside her he said, 'I didn't think
of you riding in this direction on a newly broken horse.
We've been scouring the countryside for you. Hudson is
urious that you were out on your own on Milo.'

'Huh! He's home is he? He needn't have worried
about me, Milo has been a perfect angel.'

Lee turned to ride with her. 'No, he's not home, he's
been ringing from Christchurch at least a dozen times.
He's been stirring things along over there, setting up a
olan to find your ring. I'm to pick up the boys and take
you over the hill. I'll say this for Hudson, when he gets
activated he's hard to stop, and the impossible only takes
him a little longer.'

'What do you mean?' Her eyes were sparkling.

'The wool, he's going to search the wool clip tomorrow. I bet he's been driving them bananas over
here. The insurance company has given him permission
o hire some pro's to scan the wool, and the stock and
station agents have given him one day to use the
woolstore, you've never heard the likes of it. He says he
knows it's there and he'll find it tomorrow.'

Milo, as if sensing her urgency, broke into a gallop and
outdistanced Dicer up the last long stretch to the stables.

With a glowing face she flung herself from the saddle and hugged the horse. 'I love him, I love him, and he loves me, Milo.'

'Throw a few things in a case; we'll be staying over night. I'll go and put Hudson out of his misery. He' been picturing you dragged by the stirrup, or drowned i the Haupiri. Never known him to lose his cool before became quite abusive when we couldn't find you.'

All the way over the alpine pass her heart was singing She was going to Hudson.

Lee commented, 'That ring must be worth a mint we've had full staff on it twice. When costing is done, I' bet it would have been cheaper for Hudson to hav bought you a new one.'

They went to the enormous woolstore in the morning and Serenity's eyes widened at the thousands upor thousands of bales of wool in orderly lines. She stoo watching them set up the sheets of hardboard on wool bales and waited with nerve ends tingling for the bleep o a scanner to announce the ring had been found. All da the team worked on the tables, pulling the wool across waiting for it to be scanned, then piling it into bins for the wool storemen to rebale. They had to be out by five o'clock when the security alarms would be reset, and although Hudson had narrowed the choice down to fifteen bales it looked like being a close thing.

Strangely, as the afternoon wore away, everyone go more hopeful rather than less. When Hudson's frien from the DSIR came in about four with the larges scanner ever imported, all work stopped and the excite ment was intense.

'Glad to see you, Alan,' Hudson grasped his hand and shook it vigorously. 'We're counting on you, time' running out.'

'I warned you, we're still testing its capacity. I don'

know if it will work on wool. Glad to have the opportunity to test it,' Alan warned him. 'Now, we'll run over the outsides of these unopened bales first, and see if we can get hold of something.'

Everyone waited breathlessly as the first bale was scanned, then the next, also with no result. Only one to go. On the very last side the scanner went mad and so did the team.

'Keep calm till we get in there. It could be anything. Rip it open Hudson,' Alan ordered, his eyes bright with excitement.

As the wool spewed out the bleeper kept echoing and Serenity, with pulses racing, thought she had never heard a sweeter sound.

Exultantly, Hudson handed her the ring and kissed her while everyone cheered. 'Your wedding is Wednesday, the day of the barbecue. It's all arranged.'

'That's the day after tomorrow,' Serenity gasped. 'How did you know you'd find it?'

'I knew,' he grinned wickedly. 'I said there'd be no delay, and why was I so sure? Hold out your hand, Serenity.'

As she thrust out her hand with the ring on it, Hudson took a box from his pocket and flicked the lid open, 'Snap.'

She stared down at the two identical rings, then looked at him. 'You were going to cheat if you didn't find it,' she accused.

'Of course,' he smiled triumphantly. 'Did you think I'd let anything get in the way of making you my bride? Nothing will spoil our wedding day, nothing will spoil our marriage, certainly not a little tuppeny ring.'

She couldn't help laughing with him, yet her heart was overwhelmed by his gesture . . . not counting the cost.

*

Wednesday dawned cloudless and fair, a perfect day for
her wedding. The huge marquee was erected on the
lawn, and the Canadians arrived by bus, friends and
relations by plane and cars, and Barbie was there to help
her dress.

'Oh, Serenity, you look divine, a real dreamy bride,
just exquisite. And that Hudson of yours, a real man,
just what the doctor ordered . . . my doctor.'

'Oh, you and Robbie,' Serenity smiled at her. 'How
wonderful to have you here. I still can't believe it.'

'You'd better believe it. I wouldn't have missed it for
worlds. I've never put in a morning like it, watching the
sheep dogs working and the agility of the horses, and
those cattle, they shook the ground when they thun-
dered past. The Canadians are tickled pink at being
included in such an occasion. They're just loving it, the
best day of the whole tour, they're all saying, and that's
only the morning. Well, everyone's so relaxed and
friendly—they can't help smiling, me too.'

'Some days are diamonds,' said Serenity, smiling too.

As Serenity came out on the steps on the arm of
Robert Blair, who had claimed the privilege of giving the
bride away, she heard the chatter and the laughter die
away. She looked away to where the lake sparkled blue
like a jewel in the sunshine, that's where they had met,
early one morning. She walked confidently forward to
take her place by Hudson, where the sun filtered down
through the giant trees and the chime of the bell-birds
filled the air.

The guests gathered about them in a semi-circle, and
in the midst of friends, she and Hudson exchanged their
vows. The words they had chosen themselves made it a
special service. Hudson had been right about his father,
he did indeed have a flair for arranging a splendid
occasion. No other girl would have a wedding like this,

no other girl would have a bridegroom like Hudson.

And in complete silence, the soloist's voice soared to the heavens, 'How great thou art, How great thou art', and Serenity held tightly to Hudson's hand hardly able to bear the joy of it all.

His parents were first to kiss and congratulate them, then Cam, then the whole tempo quickened as the famous Kokatahi Band started to play. Dressed in their gold-mining regalia and beating a fantastic toe-tapping rhythm on old-fashioned instruments, they lifted the mood to a new height of laughter and happiness.

Guests moved down the terraces to take crimson wine in silver goblets, slices of beef, from where the huge saddle of prime bullock turned on a spit over a glowing bed of coals of *matai* wood and it was as if time had ceased to exist.

As dusk deepened into dark, she and Hudson waltzed together in the marquee, oblivious of the crowd, lost to everyone but themselves and their love for each other.

He smiled down at her, and bent his auburn head to her fair one. 'The only way I'm going to get you out of here is to do a young Lochinvar act. This will go all night, and if we start to say goodbyes we'll never be alone together.'

He swooped her up in his arms, and strode through the cheering crowd, out past the bonfire still sending sparks into the night, and placed her in his car.

'Look at the moon, Hudson, just look at the moon.'

'The moon is always closer at Haupiri, darling, like the wind is close; like you and me, darling—always and forever, close to each other.'

Coming Next Month in Harlequin Romances!

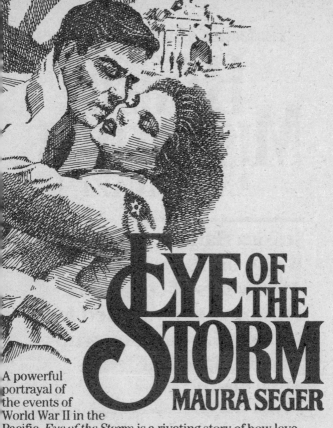

EYE OF THE STORM

MAURA SEGER

A powerful
portrayal of
the events of
World War II in the
Pacific, *Eye of the Storm* is a riveting story of how love
triumphs over hatred. Aboard a ship steaming toward
Corregidor, Army Lt. Maggie Lawrence meets Marine Sgt.
Anthony Gargano. Despite military regulations against frater-
nization, they resolve to face together whatever lies ahead....
A searing novel by the author named by *Romantic Times* as
1984's Most Versatile Romance Author.